STANDING LIONS

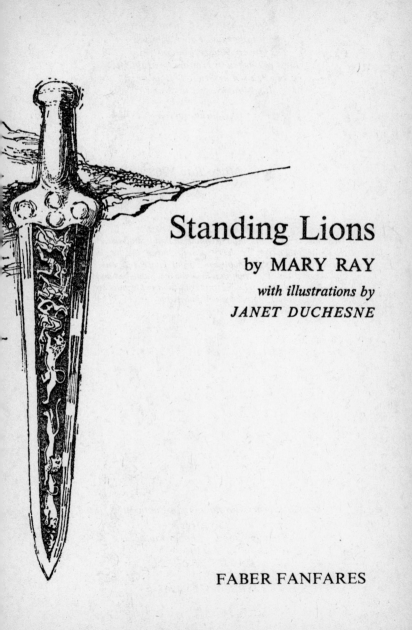

Standing Lions

by MARY RAY

with illustrations by
JANET DUCHESNE

FABER FANFARES

First published in mcmlxviii
by Faber and Faber Limited
3 Queen Square London WC1
First published in Fanfares edition 1978
Printed in Great Britain by
Jarrold & Sons Ltd, Norwich

© *Mary Ray* 1968

British Library Cataloguing in Publication Data
Ray, Mary
Standing lions. – (Faber fanfares).
I. Title
823'.9'1J   PZ7.R21015

ISBN 0–571–11267–6

For the Melians

By the same author

SONG OF THUNDER
A TENT FOR THE SUN
THE IDES OF APRIL
SWORD SLEEP
BEYOND THE DESERT GATE

LIVING IN EARLIEST GREECE

CONTENTS

1

LORD OF ARGOS

THIN, blue curtains hung at the window of the king's sleeping room. They swayed in the hot, dry air and the bar of light that lay across the floor moved with them. The sun hung above the citadel all the burning hours of the afternoon, too small and brilliant to seem to alter, for here in the plain it was already full summer. The tufts of grass and the peaflowers that grew between the stones of the great wall were withered, and the grey stalks of the asphodel stood in the meadows below like ghosts.

In the central court of the citadel the guard changed and above in the palace the moving finger of light reached up on to the king's bed. It touched Diomedes' bare leg as he lay on top of the purple coverlet and flashed into his eyes. His hand moved sleepily to brush the warmth away.

When I saw that he was awake I got up, stretching, from the stool near the door.

"It's early yet," he said, running a hand through the long, fair hair that clung damply round his face.

"No. This room faces west, not like our old place, and it will take a long while, putting on all your finery for the first time."

He looked at the garments spread ready across the cedarwood chest. "Hipponax, it seems so soon."

"I know, but how do you think your grandfather felt the day after his father's death, when he had to put the king's mantle on for the first time? Like a child playing with his father's clothes and afraid of being caught!"

"But then the old king was dead. My grandfather isn't."

He got up from the bed and went to stand at the window, looking out over the flat roofs that clustered below the citadel, and then across the golden plain to the mountains standing in a crescent of lilac and blue whose points rested on the great bay to the south.

"To the city he's dead," I said. "The gods have touched him and set him aside from ruling. Until he is himself again, if that day should ever come, as his nearest kin you are lord of Argos. The city must be ruled. Come now, I can hear the servants bringing your bath water."

He turned away from the window obediently, a tall boy, golden-brown from the long days of early summer that we had spent up in the mountains training with the other young men. There was a long graze up his left arm only two days old. I remembered how cross I had been with him that afternoon when he had not slowed his team enough for a narrow turn on the track down to the plain; I had told him he was too old to be thrown from his chariot because his mind was on something else. I did not know then that he was watching the flying cloak of my brother as he drove in haste from Argos to the valley in the western foothills where my father was steward of Dimini, the manor that had belonged to Tydeos, Diomedes' father. That was our first news of the old king's madness.

Only two days ago! I remembered that Diomedes had said nothing, at first, when Damon had given his message. He had stood a little behind the chair where my father Bias was sitting, with arms clasped tightly round himself, rubbing the bruises below the graze. My brother was covered with the dust of the valley road and his eyes were sunken into his head with lack of sleep, but he would not rest, pacing back and forth beside

10

the hearth so that his shadow flickered in the late afternoon light that came in through the doorway.

"The guard of Mecistheos can't be more than an hour behind me," he said. "He couldn't send to anyone else. For the moment it's as if King Adrastus is dead; some god has taken away the part that's human, anyway, and Argos must have a king."

"But Adrastus has a son living," said my father, his big head resting on one fist while his eyebrows knotted in the effort to see a way through the web of relationships that gather around royalty.

"Argos must have a king. Aegialus is a child, younger than Diomedes was when his own father was killed seven years ago; anyway he's with his mother's father away north of the isthmus. Diomedes is nearly grown, he can hold the land till Adrastus is well again—if that day should come."

"Where is he now, after . . . after what happened last night?" Diomedes spoke for the first time.

"Locked in the safest room of the palace with half a company of the guard outside. The king has had these fits before, but not like last night; it's a brave man who will try to disarm a madman, and a hero who will tackle the man when he is a king. Only Mecistheos in Argos could have done it, but one of the guards was dead by then, and a woman."

"Where will the king go?" asked my father.

"The word was that Mecistheos would send him north to one of the shrines across the gulf; peace may come more quickly there, and he can travel drugged in a litter."

"And so the barons looked towards Dimini and remembered that the king had at least one grandson, though his daughters and the husbands he found them are dead," I said. "Will Diomedes be a king then, or only the mouthpiece of Mecistheos?"

"I shall be a king," said Diomedes in a voice that was

unfamiliar and husky. "Otherwise Mecistheos wouldn't have sent for me. I must ride to the city tonight, and Hipponax will come with me."

So now, two days later, I was no longer the steward's son who had been part guard, part governess to the growing boy for the seven years since I had come home to Dimini at the end of my military training; now I was the cupbearer of a king.

I heard Diomedes splashing in the terracotta bath tub in the next room, then it was quieter as the servants dried and oiled him for the first banquet of his reign. By the time he came back the lamps were already lit in the sleeping room and outside the plain was dying into a purple haze. As I watched, the sun dipped between two black peaks and the last colour faded.

The servants had followed Diomedes through from the bathroom but he waved them away, suddenly impatient. I dressed him in a tunic fringed with gold and in boots of vermilion leather, intricately worked and tagged with golden chains. By themselves lay the jewels of the king, the collar of lotus shapes strung closely together, the rings of dark stone engraved with pictures of the gods, the narrow diadem of gold, beaten into a pattern of daisy flowers.

I combed back his hair, fastening it with curls of gold wire, while he picked up the dagger with the crystal knob that had been his father's and settled it in its sheath. Last of all he fastened the great blue cloak that had been his grandfather's and threw it back from his shoulders.

"It's hot," he said, as I straightened the folds; already the sweat was standing in beads along his brow.

"I know," I answered, as I turned to put on my own new tunic. "We've been as bare as two peasants these last months. The wine is newly cooled, will you drink, my lord?"

I was laughing as I spoke, kneeling to lace up my left boot, the new solemnity unfamiliar and only half meant. Then I looked up; Diomedes had gone over to the table where the wine stood ready in the pottery cooler beside the flower-shaped goblets. He poured one cup almost unmixed and stood with it in his hand smiling down at me.

I saw a king. He was young, and yet already passing me in height, and about him was a quality, a rightness—like the sheen on polished metal or the bloom on newly planed wood, something that came from the favour of the Mistress who made and strengthened all kings. And it was Diomedes. I had trained him for this, and according to the custom of the land during those years we had lived and eaten together and he had served me and been subject to me. It was strange that during all that time I had never seen that this moment would come, when he was king and it was for me to pour him wine, and drink with him only at his pleasure.

The silence, which had been more a stillness in my mind than in the room, ended as the guard outside came to attention and the door opened. Damon, my brother, who before had been no more than one of the royal guard, was now the king's captain, and this was a formal occasion. He dropped to one knee with a soft clashing of scabbard against the inlaid bronze plates of his ceremonial armour, the long crimson crest flowing over one shoulder as he bent a helmeted head to kiss the king's hand.

Diomedes put down the wine cup. For a moment his eyes met mine in a blank uncertain look, then he swallowed hard and put his head up.

"Are we ready?" he said, and led the way out of the room.

There were two stairways down from the upper galleries of the palace. One led directly into the great hall, the other into the courtyard near to the porch where the guests of the king slept, or waited for an audience. Lamps already burned along the passages and in the hands of the guards who led us, and there was a muffled sound of those who were to attend

13

the banquet coming from below, like the excited distant buzzing of bees before a thunderstorm.

The guard led us down by the more indirect way so that the king could enter the hall through the main doors. There was a pool of darkness between the pillars at the foot of the stairs, and something moved in the shadow. Damon's quick order halted the guard. A man held his torch high, one hand on the hilt of his dagger, then he laughed and stood back.

"Let me see," Diomedes said.

"It's only a child, my lord," Damon answered him. "Now who. . . ." His voice changed. "It's Philon."

"Whose child is he?"

"His father was one of your guard. Till two days ago." Damon's voice, filled with embarrassment, trailed into silence.

"Two days ago?" Diomedes said sharply. "His father is dead, and two days ago? Damon, was this the man my grandfather killed when the madness took him? And he had a son—I was not told."

"Philon has always lived in the citadel, and yet I think with so much to be done he must have been forgotten."

"Hold the torch up and let me see," said Diomedes.

All this time the boy had not moved. He was perhaps nine years old and thin, crouching, his head rigidly back against the pillar, looking straight before him. His hands hung limp across his skinny knees, and even when the king's cloak swept across his bare feet as Diomedes stood above him, he did not move.

Diomedes went down on one knee, taking the unresisting hands into his own, and then the child turned his head, peering at the face above him that was dark against the torchlight.

Diomedes' voice was so low that I could hardly hear what he said.

14

"I know how it feels, believe me, I know. I was your age when they told me what they told you. It's lonely, isn't it, and it doesn't feel true? You try to go to sleep and wake up yesterday. But Philon, it doesn't last, not like this, not unless you make it."

"It happened to you?" The boy's voice was hoarse with crying. I remembered Diomedes had not been much older when he first came into my care; a desolate child whose father had been killed away on a useless war north of the Isthmus.

"Yes," said Diomedes, still holding Philon's hands. "I was alone, but not for very long. You see, you loved your father, but now you must learn to love other people as well. That doesn't mean you must forget him, but remember, you are also a subject of the king, and you live in his palace. There's no more time to cry, because you have work to do."

"But it was the king . . . there isn't one now."

"There is. I am king and I have orders for you. Go to the kitchen, they will be busy there, but tell them to give you bread and milk with honey in it, warm milk. Then you are to go back to the barracks and you will sleep. Tomorrow I shall have work for you to do."

The child looked up in amazement, then down at the hands that still held him firmly. He dropped his head quickly to kiss them, and scrambled to his feet.

Diomedes stood up and turned to Damon. "Send a man with him, otherwise he may get overlooked."

As we entered the great hall of the palace the lords and ladies bowed low like barley before the wind, and they were gilded too as barley is when it is ripe. Diomedes paced across the dolphins and sea birds painted in the squares of the plaster floor and sat down in the king's seat against the eastern wall, looking out over this central place of the palace. It was high and square, with a raised hearth in the middle between the four tapering pillars that supported the upper galleries. The painted walls were almost hidden behind the jewel-coloured cloaks of the men and the flounced skirts of the ladies, so that the hunting party that rode out along the fresco seemed to be staring above the heads of a crowd.

One by one the lords of the council came and knelt to the king, the captains of companies and those barons from the nearer manors who had been able to reach the city in time. Diomedes, who had grown up with their sons, sat grave and

16

remote to receive their homage. Then as the last man bowed his way to his place there was a pause. Eyes turned towards the door, the steward waited to give the signal for the meal to be served, the guests began to shuffle, looking towards the couches set round the walls. Then the guard outside came once more to attention and the Lady Persea with her attendants swept into the room.

She glided more like a statue that moves than a woman, the flounces of her many-coloured skirts tinkling with ornaments of gold, her waist minute beneath a bodice so smoothly fitting that it looked as if her body and arms had been painted. The white skin of her breasts was bare, yet thickly covered with necklaces and her face was a painted mask beneath a head-dress of golden lilies. She was the old king's sister, great-aunt to Diomedes though much younger than her brother, and there was no sign of age upon her as she curtseyed to the new king. Diomedes had risen to greet her, yet she did not speak, gliding swiftly to her seat across the hearth against the west wall.

I watched her as the meal moved forward from spiced and dressed wild fowl to the great joints of meat from the day's sacrifice. A small fire burned on the hearth between the king and the princess and through the heat that rose from it in the still night air, her face wavered and changed. She was high priestess of the Mistress in Argos and tonight she did not look to me as if she was fully human herself.

Now I had my new duties to perform. I served Diomedes from the great dishes that the squires carried from table to table, although he was too excited to eat much. Close to him my brother sat, his long legs spread, eyes watchful, missing no movement of the guard, no grouping of guests around the scarlet pillars. He was young for his responsibility, and the crown was not so secure on Diomedes' head that he could afford to be unwary.

Close to Damon was Mecistheos, governor of the citadel, to look at a tall, hard man, approaching middle age, his beard dark beneath the deep-cleft lines on his face; in the knowledge of his loyalty we had come down to the citadel and slept one night already in safety under its roofs. Somewhere in this hall there must be treachery. It was too much to hope that the king could change as easily in a kingdom as a man takes off one cloak and puts on another; I wondered what the thoughts were behind the wine-bright eyes below me.

Across the room the Lady Persea gestured to one of her attendants and the small table beside her chair was moved back. All round us the greasy dishes were cleared while a troupe of tumblers somersaulted around the hearth to the rhythm of a drum. My eyes went back to the young attendant who stood beside the lady's chair as I stood beside the king. She was young, slim and brown-haired, in a saffron-skirted dress sewn with turquoise beads, her head-dress twisted with turquoise and gold.

In the last years I had not been often in the place. Diomedes lived as much on the land that had been his father's as with the old king, and since the last summer there had been the long months of military training that every boy of noble blood must receive; yet I remembered this girl, there was something about the way she moved as she bent to pour wine that I had known a long time.

I knew her as she turned across the room and looked at me. Perhaps she had felt my gaze, for we were near kin. She was my cousin Chryseis from our home at Dimini. The year since I had seen her last had changed and ripened her out of all recognition. I wished that it was some village wedding so that I could leave Diomedes and go to speak with her, but we both had our duties to perform. Later I would tell her the news from home.

Diomedes held up his golden cup. The wine he had drunk

in the hall had been well watered, yet he was flushed with the heat and weight of his robes.

"How much longer?" he asked me quietly. "I begin to envy the child who is sent to bed before the party's over."

"If you go now it will stop for everyone!" I said, smiling. "Not very long now. I think the bard from Troizen is preparing to sing, and by then everyone will have had enough to drink."

Even as I spoke I saw Diomedes look past me. There was a sound from outside louder than the wellbred voices of the guests and the tumblers' music. A chariot was being driven into the outer courtyard.

Mecistheos bowed to Diomedes and walked swiftly out, with the dancers parting before him. The drum beat faltered and stopped so that I heard his voice outside. Then he came back through the doorway, and with him a young captain in a dust-stained tunic, helmetless, with a long shallow cut oozing on his right arm. Diomedes stood up as the young man fell on his knees before him.

"Lord King," he gasped in a voice rough with pain. "I come from the garrison at the mouth of the river. Men of Tiryns crossed the fords at dusk. The fortress is taken and they are burning the standing crops. We could not tell how great their strength is, but they could reach Argos before dawn."

2

THE KING RIDES SOUTH

IT was first light on the southern bastion of the citadel. Below in the town cocks were crowing and I could hear the precise sound of a donkey's hooves echoing in the narrow place between the houses at the foot of the walls. Damon pointed towards the sea, invisible still in a pearly haze.

"Look, that's more than mist."

A darker thread was rising towards the bright air high above.

Diomedes said, "It's not a new fire. Whatever's burning there has been alight for some hours and it's nearly back as far as the fords. Kaletor has held them."

He looked at Mecistheos, seeking agreement. For a long moment the tall man peered through the dawn haze, then he said, "You're right, my lord. It seems that we have a little time after all, and perhaps my manor near the sea is safe."

I heard a rustle spread back among the captains of fifty behind us, and then, more faintly, along the walls where the garrison of Argos stood to their arms.

"Kaletor knows that we shall expect word from him at dawn, and even if the smoke is deceiving us there will be some warning of an attack," said Damon. "Shall I order half the men to stand down for breakfast?"

"Yes, very well, and now I must find myself some armour that fits," said Diomedes. "Send me word when Kaletor's messenger comes."

The palace had woken behind us as the sun's rays touched it; the clatter of chariots and a neighing of horses came from the lower courtyard. A procession of men spaced like ants carried baskets of grain from the great magazines below the palace. I could hear the hammering of smiths, and a stench of scorching hide mixed with the smell of new bread. The great hall was empty except for a knot of officers eating breakfast on their feet, fully armed. They bowed to Diomedes as he strode ahead of me to the staircase. Now Argos was at war and the pretty ladies and painted robes had gone.

The chief armourer was waiting in the king's apartments. For the last months Diomedes had worn no more than light practice armour, now he must face an enemy unprepared. He was tired from a night with little sleep and the strain made him irritable.

The man brought forward a cuirass of soft leather, padded with felt and sewn with bronze disks. "My lord, I think this should fit you well enough."

Diomedes looked at it with distaste. "Where is the bronze armour of my grandfather?"

"He was taller than you," I said. "There hasn't been time to take out enough of the plates to make it fit."

"When I'm older, I know!" His voice was bad-tempered; then he saw dismay in the armourer's eyes and the corners of his mouth twitched. "Why are you always right, Hipponax? It would be mad to wear it untried in this summer heat. Very well, let me try the other."

He dropped his cloak on the bed and unfastened his belt. The leather armour, light and flexible as a fish's scales, fitted close to the body. I fastened the straps down the back and he wriggled his tunic smooth over the shoulders; the armourer came forward to adjust it professionally.

"Is the right armhole easy? There's no strain as you stretch forward?"

Diomedes buckled on his sword belt and practised drawing the blade quickly. "No, that seems all right. Now for the rest."

There were leather and metal leg guards that fitted down over heavy boots, and a small round shield on a leather strap that could be hung over the shoulder ready to swing down quickly on to the left arm. Diomedes walked the length of the room in all this and then came back, treading heavily, already very warlike and in a rather better temper.

The armourer picked up a bundle wrapped in linen; he had the look of a man who is about to produce something that he knows will give pleasure.

"Your helmet, my lord." He let the linen slip, and Diomedes stepped forward to take the strange and beautiful helmet from him.

22

It was made of boars' teeth, many rows of them, over-lapping round the leather lining like the half-closed petals of a flower. Other rows protected the neck and curved down into cheek guards, milky white in the warm morning sun save for a flaring red crest. I had seen it before on the head of the old king and knew that it was many generations old, made in the time when the wild boars fed nearer the plain. There was none other like it still in use in the city and few in all Argos. Diomedes put it on and fastened the chin strap.

"It's light," he said. "Will it really turn a blow?"

"Yes, and with hardly a mark to show for it. You could wear it all day and not be weary; the sign of the boar was the crest your father wore."

"So it was! I must have a new shield made when there's time." He took the helmet off and gave it to me, turning as a guard appeared in the doorway.

"Lord Kaletor's messenger has just reached the lower courtyard, Lord King."

"Are the officers still on the south bastion?"

"Yes, my lord."

"Have the messenger brought to us there."

A bowl with broken bread and cheese stood on the rampart and a squire was ready with a jug of watered wine. Diomedes began to eat absentmindedly, holding out a cup to be filled. Damon, Mecistheos and their captains were talking among themselves, looking back from time to time at the smoke far down the valley. The messenger came up the stairway from the courtyard two at a time, and then hesitated, as if uncertain to which of the men he should speak. Almost imperceptibly the lords of Argos moved aside so that Diomedes, the half-eaten bread still in his hand, stood in the centre of the group.

The young man dropped on one knee, too inexperienced yet for his face to hide his thoughts as he first saw Diomedes' youth, and then the new armour and the conviction with which he wore it.

"Stand up," said Diomedes. "Did they give you anything to drink down below?"

The messenger shook his head.

"Here then, finish this, or your throat will be too dry to talk."

He held out his own cup. The young man took it in his dusty hands, eyes wide with astonishment, and the lords settled themselves against the ramparts to hear his report.

"The men from Tiryns crossed the ford in strength," he said. "Now they hold all the land back towards the sea, but nothing further north. Lord Kaletor came up with their scouts a short march from the fords and turned them back with a little fighting. He has pitched camp in the olive groves and lower hayfields of the Lord Mecistheos, next to the river. Our scouts say that King Leander is with his men. Lord Kaletor believes that he will give battle today as soon as the heat slackens and his full force is over the river. King Leander is well prepared, with at least seven hundreds of men and many chariots. My lord begs the king to come with all speed and as many men as he can muster."

Diomedes did not speak at once. He looked slowly at the men around him, then down over the citadel to the clustering town below, riding up out of the summer-dry fields of the plain like a great ship. To the east where the olives grew more thickly the line of the river was lost among the reed banks and the little farms. It marked the boundary of Argos; across and far up into the mountains was the land of Tiryns, while at the head of the valley Mycenae, citadel of the High King over all the lands south-east of the isthmus, squatted on its little hill between the twin peaks and watched all that was done from the foothills to the sea.

The High King was overlord of all the little kingdoms, of

24

Argos and Tiryns, Nemea to the north and Troizen east over the ridges that separated us from the greater sea. The kingdoms squabbled among themselves, choosing their own rulers, but when the High King fought they rode with him and when the uproar between them was too great, he came down from his castle to give justice. Or that was how it had been in the past. Now Mycenae had come to lesser days, the royal line had been broken, and the best the little kingdoms could hope for was no news from Mycenae.

Diomedes turned back to the south, screwing up his eyes against the sun. Already all detail had gone, lost in its colourless bright glare. The polished armour of the captains hurt the eyes, and sweat was beginning to run under my tunic.

The king brushed his hair back and said, "Two hours' march to the fords, Lord Mecistheos. How many of our men can reach there in time?"

"Kaletor has his own hundred with him and those we sent last night. We can't leave Argos unguarded, and the men from the north who have already reached us have marched all night."

"And those from the western valleys?"

"The land is marshy near the bay, so they must go by the inland road. It will be further for them than for us. By two hours after noon five hundred from here can have reached Kaletor and by evening our numbers should be equal. Yet the battle may have been lost or won by then."

"And chariots?"

"Not more than forty."

"Damon, those of the men who are ready should march as soon as possible, before the sun is really high, with those from the north. They can rest before the battle if there's time. Better to fight tired than not be there at all, and anyway if Leander sees us in full strength it may not come to fighting."

Damon went down the stairs into the courtyard. Soon there

25

was a distant shouting of orders and the blowing of a horn.

Diomedes turned to us. "But why should Leander do it? The land he holds goes far back into the mountains, and it's as rich as ours."

"Lord Diomedes," said Mecistheos. "There are many kings in the valleys; with Argos and Tiryns joined that would be one less. Perhaps Leander grows restless and wonders why one man from a cleft in the rock should rule us all. In time he might be strong enough to challenge the High King Thyestes himself, and if those are his thoughts then he must start somewhere."

"His plans must have been ready and he's moved fast then. It's scarcely two full days since my grandfather's illness; less since we sent him north to the sanctuary of the god."

"King Leander is a very young man, perhaps he's impatient. He has been king himself for only two years, though that may have been long enough for it to have come to feel easy. He may be looking for more excitement after the years of peace."

"But why on my land! Still, I'd like to meet him, we. . . ." He did not finish the sentence and the words hung in the air between him and the older men. I realized then that inside I was still as much in awe of Mecistheos as I had been when I was a new recruit in the guard ten years before. How did he seem to Diomedes, when even I must seem hopelessly unaware of how it felt to be a king, and so young.

Mecistheos looked down at the snake's head of foot soldiers that had appeared beyond the houses, raising the dust on the southern road.

"Before sundown you may indeed be face to face, lord king."

The gilded royal chariot was already waiting below in the courtyard. I inspected the axles and the lashings of the yoke bar. The servants had already stowed my armour neatly

26

away against the side supports, for I should drive Diomedes into battle. While he spoke to the steward of the palace, giving him the last orders for the safeguarding of all we should leave behind us, I went back once more to the king's apartments. My cloak lay across the low bed in the alcove beside the door. Slaves had tidied away the other signs of the king's arming. The room looked as it had the first morning we had entered it. The first morning! It was only yesterday.

If the battle today went against us we might not see this room again. Perhaps the young king of Tiryns would sleep here. The great walls of the citadel had stood so long that perhaps her kings were really no more to her than the vine flowers that open for one day and then die.

I turned away quickly and clattered down the stairs without looking back. The palace servants had gathered to watch us go; their faces were interested, perhaps pitiful, but who were we that any of them should weep yet for our danger? The place was still numb from the horror of the old king's madness.

I saw Diomedes looking about for me and went across to the chariot. He had been holding his helmet; now he put it on while I mounted and took the reins from the groom. Then there was an eddy in the crowd, low down among their legs. A small, scarlet face appeared, and then a child's body, worming its way to the front. Diomedes paused, surprised, the strap half buckled; then he walked back quickly to the edge of the crowd.

"Philon!"

The child wriggled free and stood before him. "You told me to come for my orders." The voice was high-pitched, reproachful.

Diomedes smiled. "So I did, you were right to remind me. Philon, you see how it is, for the next few days I won't be in the palace so that you could serve me yourself, but there is something you can do for me all the same. You know the stables where the horses are kept?"

"Yes of course I do . . . my lord."

"Have you seen the horses I came with two days ago, two bays, one of them with a white star? They aren't trained to pull a heavy war chariot, so they've been left behind. I've driven them for a long time, Philon, and now they'll be frightened in a strange place. Will you help to look after them for me, and talk to them?"

"Oh yes, my lord!" The child bowed very low and then ducked back into the crowd. Those who were nearest and had heard what was said were smiling as Diomedes jumped up beside me in the chariot.

I looked up once before we entered the dark tunnel below the gatehouse through the inner walls, where the women craned out from the windows of the palace; it seemed that the cheering behind us had taken on a warmer note. Then the hooves rang in the enclosed place as we skidded across the deep grooves in the stone paving outside the gate and followed the road down into the town.

The people called to us as we rode between the tall houses, and children ran with the dogs that snapped at our wheels so that it took me all my skill to avoid them. Then we came out into the first of the olive groves, the branches nearest the road white with the dust that still hung in the air from the men who had marched that way not long before.

For the first time war spears stood in the holder close to Diomedes' hand on the rim of the chariot. I wondered what he was thinking; the noise of the wheels in the baked ruts of the road made talking almost impossible. I, who had thought I knew him so well, had never seen him look quite as he did now. There was the weariness first that had never quite left us since our night ride down from the mountains; I had ridden to war before and knew that this was how it always was, that battles are fought by tired men and that the leader who wins is the one who can think most clearly through the grey fog of exhaustion and the pain of wounds. Diomedes was learning it now and it was a hard lesson to come to, so early in this his first command. He would not fight for the first time well back among the squires, but in the centre of the charge. Yet he was the son of a prince, one of the wandering lords who had ruled my people through their generations, and I who was a grown man dreaded what lay ahead of us towards the sea in a way which I saw now he would never understand. It was more than the difference between experience and ignorance. I understood now more clearly than ever before that I was a man of the land, my father was Diomedes' steward and my joy was in seeing a ripe harvest carried and young sheep safe among the rocks, not to hear the bard sing of the manors I had destroyed. I would fight for these things that I loved, and for this boy, but not for fighting itself. It seemed that there was need for men of both sorts in a kingdom.

The road swung down towards the river, Diomedes gripped my shoulder to steady himself, looking back at the chariots that followed us, and the tail of marching men, then he drank from the water bottle strapped near his hand and passed it to me. The king of Argos seemed to have withdrawn a little, he was easy with me, and yet I thought for one moment as the heat beat down and the road shimmered ahead that if we spoke, it would not be in the same language.

3

THE ORCHARDS OF MECISTHEOS

As we neared the orchards of Mecistheos the country became empty and there were no more children staring from the little farms. The people had all been ordered into the villages by their elders, the cattle driven to safety, and now the fields lay quiet in the sun with the corn standing half cut as the reapers had left it.

A little after the hottest time of the day we rode into the camp of Kaletor, captain of the thousand of Argos. There had been no time to set up a proper headquarters and no need; he had taken the barns and stockyards of Mecistheos' manor. To the east was the river among its osiers, towards the sea were the hay fields, parched and empty, sloping down to a garden near a spring with rows of vegetables and a few old trees. Beyond, the ground rose again towards the village around the fort that had guarded the fords, hidden in its olive groves. No smoke rose now, but a glint of armour and a movement of men showed now and then below the silver-grey shadow of the trees on the hillside.

Already the stockyard looked like an army camp many weeks old. Horses, restless with heat and the clouds of flies, were tethered in lines near the well, where there was any shade. There were wounded men in the largest barn, with the women of the farm moving among them; a drift of smoke and a shout of laughter came from the cooking fires on the threshing floor.

The hundreds from the western villages were coming in; most of the other men rested where they could. They seemed cheerful enough, polishing armour, plaiting back their long hair, or curled sleeping, away from passing feet. Only here and there a young face masked in dust looked straight ahead and did not seem to hear what was being said by the men around. There was a constant coming and going, captains striding among the few hens that had still not been caught, dogs everywhere, orderlies carrying water; movement and heat and a smell of squashed grass and herbs, horse dung, sweat, and the sour latrines of men who are soon to fight a battle.

The confusion parted before me as I drove the well-trained horses of the old king Adrastus straight up to the vine-covered porch where Kaletor and his captains were sitting. Grooms ran to the horses' heads, and the chariot was hardly still before Diomedes had jumped down and strode across to them.

The general gave a short businesslike bow and said, "You are none too soon, Lord King."

Dignity was not Kaletor's quality, he was a man of power, short, bullnecked and barrel-chested with a lumpy face baked brown under the mat of hair that jutted in alarming tufts out of his helmet and round his chin. I had seen him throw a man taller than himself out of a room with the flat of his hand, and move a bogged-down chariot by turning round and shoving with the great muscles of his back. Now he had a king who was only a boy and an army disorganised by a sudden attack; I wondered what he would do.

"Is there more news of Leander? When do you think that he'll attack?" asked Diomedes.

Kaletor put one hand on his shoulder and guided him to the end of the terrace where there was a view over the orchards of the far hillside.

"Look over there; we don't need scouts to tell us those men'll move soon. See, they can't stay still, pushed forward by the ones behind, and driving their officers mad."

Diomedes grinned, the distant movements did look like a pot coming to the boil. "And us?" he asked.

"Now that's a different matter. Let the men rest when they can, I say, as any captain with experience would. Don't get them lined up in the sun to have time to think what they're doing and lose courage. I've had it done to me. You look at a little rock and start thinking 'I may be dead before I get that far.' Lord King, we're not as many as I'd like, but we can make a show of it and it looks as if we'll have to."

A scout ran up through the cluster of men below the terrace and spoke urgently to Kaletor's second in command.

"The Tiryenian chariots are forming up over the hill, Lord King," he called.

Kaletor grinned and rubbed a fly off his nose. "Leander can't sit still. Young men, young men, it's hot yet to be fighting, dawn or dusk's what I like." Then he looked at Diomedes quizzically, still rubbing his nose. "Are we ready, my lord?"

"Direct the battle line as you would have done if I hadn't reached here in time," Diomedes said. "I shall learn more quickly that way."

Kaletor's eyelids drooped, I could see that he was pleased. "Good lad," he said very quietly. "Well then, we'll advance in column half-way down to the spring, no point in straggling out all across the hillside; then divide both ways into line of battle; the captains know their places. Where's Gelanor?"

"Here." The herald jumped down from a chariot scarcely less splendid than that of the king. Kaletor looked across at Diomedes.

"The father of Leander was the friend of my grandfather, Adrastus. Remind him of that, Gelanor," said Diomedes. "And ask him why he greets me on the first day of my reign with a gift of slaughtered peasants and burning barns. We have no quarrel with Tiryns, but if need be we will clean our own land and then cross the fords ourselves to root out the weeds that have seeded in our fields."

The herald, a tall golden-haired man, settled his helmet with its trailing plume and raised his spear in salute; he seemed to like his errand. "The lion cub of Tiryns and the young boar are well matched," he said, and wheeled his chariot in a smother of white dust.

"Time to mount, my Lord," said Kaletor, grunting as his squire buckled on his ancient, battered armour. "Memnon of the western manors has command of the right wing, and I take the left, that leaves the centre for you." He smiled again, watching to see how Diomedes would take this.

I could feel in the boy the pleasant tenseness of one who is sparring with someone against whom he is properly matched. "Of course," he said. "I shall get the best view from there. I told you I wanted to learn. Damon and my guard will ride with me."

The last of our foot soldiers passed through the stockyard, followed by the line of chariots with the knights whose duty it was to take them into battle. Diomedes fastened the boar's-tusk helmet and threw back his cloak. It was hard to see the distant wood now for the fine red dust from the hay fields thrown up by the marching men.

Our chariot stood ready. I picked up my own small shield and settled it over my shoulder with hands that were slippery with sweat. My heart sounded loud beneath the padded armour, the leather already darkened across my back in the merciless glare. The chariots of the left wing crunched and slid past over the baked ruts of the cart track; I noticed the women standing silently before the barn, and a wounded man propped up on his elbow to see us go. Nobody waved now.

Fear had been with me all the hours since the first messenger had gasped his warning in the great hall of the palace. Now the smouldering uneasiness with which a man can still sleep and eat flamed into a moment of panic. I had forgotten it was always like this. As I bent low over the reins to twist them behind me in the knot a charioteer uses when he must guide his horses by the shifting weight of his body, my stomach churned and my legs were trembling.

Diomedes jumped up beside me. I took three long breaths to quiet my belly and straightened up to look at him.

His teeth were white against the brown skin as he gave me the glance of someone who is not apprehensive, only overwhelmingly curious. Then the men behind us began to sing the battle song of Argos, the chariot ahead moved forward and I drove the team down across the hillside towards the valley and whatever waited for us there.

Kaletor had halted well above the spring. Our foot soldiers stood in a double line of men armed with leather and bronze; behind them were as many more with shields of wicker-work and felt caps on their heads. The brown-red swathe across the trampled hay seemed very thin. The horses wheeled to left and right while Kaletor waited beside us for Gelanor and the Tirynian herald. The two teams, side by side, thundered back up the hillside. The man in the saffron of Tiryns bowed from his elaborately mounted chariot and addressed himself to Kaletor.

"Leander, King of the land south of Mycenae, greets the captains of Argos. He has no wish to kill those who are to be his subjects, but if honour must be satisfied, let the Lord Kaletor choose out a champion, and after one of our warriors has disarmed him, the king will come to receive the homage of Argos."

"And if not?"

"Then Leander must come himself, and your fields will be stained a deeper red by sunset."

34

Kaletor was silent and Diomedes leaned forward, his knuckles white on the chariot rail.

"The blood of Argos will defend the fields from which the Mistress made it grow! Tell that to your king."

The herald swung his team away without a word and Gelanor reined in beside Kaletor. "Leander of Tiryns is young but his looks are grim today, and his men are well armed. Look, Lord King, his line is ready."

"Do we charge, or do we stand firm?" Diomedes had to shout above the distant cheering of the Tirynians.

"Our chariots are fewer than his, we must hold for as long as possible and then use them where the attack is fiercest. We should bring the foot soldiers further down towards the spring, where the ground is steeper and they will have the advantage. The Mistress strengthen your arm, Lord King."

Kaletor gave Diomedes a long look under his eyebrows and seemed to approve of what he saw, then his chariot raced off to its position on the left wing. Diomedes raised his spear and let it fall, and the whole line of our foot soldiers moved forward in a slow, uneven wave. Across on the other slope there was dust and shouting, and already the thunder of advancing chariots. Half-way to the spring Diomedes signalled again and the line wavered to a halt along most of its length, but part of the right wing still moved on.

Diomedes cried in a voice that rang above the heads of the restless men and the nervous clatter of the horses, "Memnon, hold!"

My brother Damon, silent in the chariot on our right, gave one of his rare laughs and shouted, "Diomedes of Argos, Diomedes of the loud war-cry!"

All down the line the answer rang out. "For Argos and Diomedes of the loud war-cry."

Diomedes turned to laugh in my face and my heart caught fire from his. I raised my arm to greet my brother and forgot tomorrow that might come but not for me, and the churning in my belly. I was a warrior of Argos and of a new king. The men of Tiryns had passed the spring now. They had almost reached our left wing, where the ground was less steep.

The rest of their line had slowed and was wavering. The chariots bunched a little way back, waiting to see if we would charge first and lose the advantage of the ground. Leander should have been in the centre of the line but I couldn't see him. Diomedes leaned far forward, tense as a coiled spring, as the enemy line paused just in range to throw their first spears. I remember the ugly hiss they made, and the sudden grove that sprang up between the two lines where many had fallen short; then Diomedes had raised his arm again and the ragged line to left and right of us poured forward.

In the next moments of shattering noise, the first screaming, clanging armour, yelling men beside themselves with fear or fury, I fought with my horses, holding back with all my strength to prevent them charging down into the heaving mass below.

"Hipponax, there!" Diomedes grasped my arm. The fighting was splitting into irregular groups, and through them the chariots of Leander were advancing; close below the weight of the Tirynian foot were pushing our own back.

Diomedes looked quickly back up the hillside and signalled a second time. The war-cry of Argos sounded again and I drove straight for the thickest part of the battle. Out of the corner of my eye I saw Diomedes poise himself, spear back, and beyond him the horses of Damon galloping level with us, the captain of the guard on the king's unprotected side.

The men ahead scattered and close before us were three of the enemy chariots. I drove for the nearest; the spearpoint of its black-bearded captain seemed to rush towards us, then it veered to the right as the charioteer threw his weight to one side to turn the off-side wheel from a boulder hidden in the

36

grass. The axle tilted and the thrust went wide. Diomedes' point caught him in the hollow below the right armpit, then the shaft was pulled from his hands by the speed of passing. I slashed to my left at the helmet of a man who jumped at the horses and then we were out in the open.

I shouted at the team, straining on the reins to turn them as they danced on their hind legs while Diomedes seized the second spear from the holder. The bearded man hung over the rail of the chariot, the spear still trailing from his side; it lay tilted up with one wheel still spinning while the charioteer tried to cut the horses loose. Damon's helmet rose above a tangle of fighting men.

"Back," shouted Diomedes.

I drove through the nearest gap in the line. Up the hill a captain in our crimson struggled alone in his chariot while a Tirynian came up on his unprotected side. We galloped to head him off. Diomedes swung his shield across us both as it swerved to meet us, and an arrow sang through the rising dust.

"Achates the bowman!" I shouted in his ear. He nodded and swung his spear arm back.

Another arrow whined between us and Diomedes jerked to one side. Then he aimed for the driver, a difficult throw across the horses' backs. The point took him in the thigh above the rim of the chariot, then our left wheel locked with his as the man dropped the reins, grasping his wound.

Diomedes had only his sword now. Achates dropped his bow to a man running beside him and drew his own. I heard a war-cry behind us, "Leander! Leander!"

The cloud of dust that now hid all but the nearest part of the battle line seemed to be sweeping back up the hill and from its centre burst a team of golden horses and a captain all in bronze, burning in the afternoon sun. Achates answered the cry, "Leander."

37

I saw that we were surrounded, and in the moment after I had looked for one cold instant at death in the stubble beneath the hooves of my own team, Diomedes shouted again, "Argos and the Mistress."

I jerked the reins so that the wheel hubs broke loose, hoping that the lynch pin had not gone as well, and Achates' next blow went wide; then we drove towards Leander of Tiryns.

There was a distant shouting back up the hillside. Were Leander's men behind us up at the farm? Then a horn blew with loud insistent blasts. I checked our speed a little, Diomedes looked over his shoulder, and Leander lowered the point of his spear. All down the field, among the smashed green of the vegetable plots where the knots of saffron and crimson fighting men could be seen through the dust, a hush fell. A single team was careering madly towards us, while the driver waved the white wand of a herald. At the edge of the

battle among the wrecked chariots and the first of the tumbled bodies, he drew rein.

"Where are the kings of Argos and Tiryns?" he cried in a voice that cracked with emotion.

Leander's chariot moved forward a few paces, uncertainly.

"Kings of the land, Diomedes, Leander, hear me," cried the herald again. "Thyestes the High King has come down from Mycenae. His men are burning everything before them, and they are coming on both sides of the river."

Leander's horses paced slowly closer to us. I saw the young king bend forward, his spear unaimed but ready, eyes watchful for a move to left or right. I turned Diomedes' chariot back down the slope as Kaletor clattered up from our left wing and Damon ran on foot to stand at our horses' heads.

"Now speak again," Diomedes commanded the herald. "Who sent you?"

"The lord Mecistheos. Certain word of an attack from the north came at noon, though even before then we had seen the smoke of burning fields. We thought it was the men of Tiryns till the wind shifted and we could see fire on both sides of the river."

Leander settled his spear back in its holder. "Diomedes, we are fighting the wrong battle on the wrong hillside. It seems that an enemy of both of us lies further north. Shall we ride together?"

4

LION KINGS

THE combined armies marched north during the night. Our men were so weary that at midnight we rested for a few hours in the olive groves north of Argos and then came at dawn for a second time to the bitter smell of scorched cornland and smoke from burning farms that darkened the sunrise. That day and the next we hunted our enemy among the orchards and the small watercourses; there was no battle, no charge of chariots, as we cleared the land acre by acre on both sides of the river; the army of Thyestes seemed more concerned to destroy than to advance. We fought only once, when a column of chariots came behind us the second day, breaking suddenly from a hillside that we thought was clear. Then I heard Diomedes' war-cry again, and there were swords to be cleaned and bodies left among the tall reeds that swung above the road.

The second night we cleared the last of them from the most northern manor on our land, where the road turned towards the east and Mycenae. We attacked and they fell back. It seemed a strange way of fighting to me, to make such a challenge and then not to push it home. It was not that Mycenae lacked men, her standing army was easily as strong as those of Argos and Tiryns together. I did not understand and I think Kaletor was puzzled as well; though Diomedes in his inexperience could not tell yet the difference between the weariness that comes from hard conflict, and the exhaustion that is caused by sleepness nights and the confusion of a divided attack.

When it was over, before another dawn, I came back from seeing to the horses to find Diomedes kneeling beside a small fire, his tunic—split across one shoulder—pushed round his waist so that he could bathe a long graze on the side of his neck. The light that flickered redly on his bare skin came from the burning roofbeams of the ruined hall across a courtyard littered with men, sleeping or wounded. The rafters trailed criss-cross through the rubble piled on the blackened floor; crests of flame still ran up the charred wood and spirted from the settling embers. Diomedes' hair was thick with dust and his eyes had dark marks around them.

"Where's Gelanor?" he asked, pitching his voice low.

"At the overseer's house down in the village; it's the only one with a roof left. His mother and the other women are there."

"I suppose this manor is his now, and it's only a smoking ruin with his father dead somewhere under it."

"Maybe, but we are alive, and Thyestes' men are back beyond the river!"

He gave a great sigh, part exhaustion, part relief. "They are, and I don't know how it was done."

A guard's challenge, quickly hushed, sounded through the broken archway to the stables. Leander of Tiryns, still in his armour of overlapping bronze plates, came from the shadows and stood above us by the little fire.

He was still very young, not two years older than Diomedes, but the lines of dearly-won experience were already as deeply cut into his face as those of a man. He was not tall, slightly built but strong, with dark hair trimmed at his shoulders like a peasant and heavy dark brows a bar above his grey eyes.

He smiled down at Diomedes, swinging his helmet in one hand, and pushed the boy's head to one side to see the wound.

"It's not deep?"

"No, only a graze. One fingerbreadth higher and the helmet would have taken all of it. Is everything quiet?"

"Yes, and the guards are awake. A water rat won't cross the river tonight." He put down the helmet and began to fumble with the straps of his breastplate.

I knelt to undo the thongs that fastened his leg armour and

he thanked me with the courtesy he showed to all who served him.

"Are you really going to rest at last?" asked Diomedes, looking up with something like hero worship in his eyes.

"My lord of Argos, I am not a God, and I'm not so young a king that I imagine I must do everything myself! Achates has the watch."

"He nearly killed me yesterday, no, it was three days ago!"

"I nearly killed you myself, and then what would have happened to Tiryns and Argos? Diomedes, Thyestes saved us from a great foolishness and we should be grateful to him for that much, but why must our people die so that we can learn?"

"Why must we fight before we can be friends? Because we're still children, I suppose."

"It's a long while since I was a child," said Leander, yawning and slipping his armour to the ground with a soft clashing of bronze plates. He stretched, pushing back his hair, then his right hand went to his thigh in an unconscious movement I had noticed before, like a man rubbing a strained muscle.

He saw my glance and smiled, embarrassed. "It aches sometimes."

"What does?" asked Diomedes, wrapped now in his cloak and leaning against a pile of torn cushions from the hall.

"It's an old wound in my leg." He turned away, but as he knelt, reaching out his hands to the comfort of the dying flames in the dawn chill, the padded tunic fell to one side and a great double scar showed clearly where a spear or sword had pierced right through.

"Leander, how did you get that and still live?" breathed Diomedes.

The young man turned his head. "Where have you been, my friend, that you haven't heard the story of Leander the twice-wounded?"

44

"In Dimini, west in the mountains, and from there Tiryns was a long way off. Tell me now. No, that's not fair, you should sleep while you can."

"Sleep? There are some wearinesses that do not loose themselves as easily as that." Then his voice changed and his face relaxed so that for a moment he looked no more than his real age. "And Diomedes, how long is it, I wonder, since I talked to a friend who wasn't more my father's age than my own!"

He settled himself by the fire and picked up Diomedes' boars'-tooth helmet. The bowl of water stood where I had left it and he began to wash the blood away from the neck piece, working slowly, his head bent as he spoke.

"Your father died, didn't he, when you were quite small. Do you remember him?"

"Not too well. Only as someone I loved and wanted to please, who punished me when I was naughty."

"There's the difference, you see. My father lived until I was almost as old as you are now, and I hope never to hate another man as I hated him."

"Even when you were a child?"

"Even then. A prince of Tiryns isn't trained as other children are. He must be perfect. Always he must work harder, his arrows must fly as far as those of boys who are two years older than he is; he must drive a chariot team that a man may fight to control, and if he hurts himself he must never cry. Worst of all, he is never for one hour alone to be lazy on the long summer days with other children or to waste his time and laugh. I lived sixteen years like this, and then one day out hunting in the eastern hills a boar charged away from the nets, the circle broke, and for a moment there was no one near me. I was deep in a thicket of thorn above the lair before I thought what I was doing, and then it was too late to go back."

"You stayed in the hills alone?"

45

"All summer. My training had made me strong, and I watched them beat the lower slopes for me day by day, changing my hiding place as the game does. If I'd been wise I would have gone east across the mountains, further even than my father's arm could reach, but I wasn't used to thinking for myself, and the fascination of looking down through the summer heat at Tiryns and my father's shame was too great."

Leander put the helmet down and clenched his hands together between his knees.

"Then he caught you at last?" asked Diomedes, as the silence lengthened.

"Yes, it was just at dawn, and I was tired. The dogs woke me, and I was too sleepy to do more than run. I made an easy target."

"That was when you were wounded?"

"It's not easy to believe, is it? A man hunting his son with war hounds! Yes, I think my father would have rather had me dead than free. When the first of them reached me I jumped for the branches of a great pine tree. The spear passed through my leg and pinned me there like a rat on a barn door."

Diomedes stretched out his hand, half afraid, and touched the great puckered scar. "I don't know how you didn't die."

"Neither do I, except that I fainted from the loss of blood and had a rest from pain. I don't remember the trek back to the citadel, only my father's look as I lay face down on a litter in the courtyard. Then I was ill a long time, most of the winter, and I was closely guarded. That was when I came to know Achates the bowman, he was one of my father's captains. So that was the first wound."

"But the spear pieced you in two places; I thought that was what you meant."

"You might well have done so, but you never knew my father. He had captured me and I was safe in the citadel of

46

Tiryns, but I hadn't been punished yet for his wounded pride. A day came in spring when I was nearly strong again, pacing my room and longing to be out under the sky even if it meant a return to the old ways of my training. My father sent for me. I stood before him in the great hall of Tiryns while his healer pronounced me well again. I thought it was all over. Then I saw his eyes as he watched me; they were hot, as a hawk's are before it makes a kill. Diomedes, the hall of Tiryns is like other halls, with four pillars painted red. I thought as the guards tied me to one of them that it was a good thing, because the plaster would not be stained by my blood."

Diomedes was staring at him in silence. "Lord Leander," I said, leaning forward into the light. "After all the pain of your wound your father still had you flogged?"

"When there is time to bathe and sleep in a bed you will see proof that he did," said Leander in a voice that was thin and quiet. "Then I was ill again, and before I was well my father died."

"Just then? How did it happen?"

"It was an accident, the axle of his chariot broke. Achates told me what happened."

"He told you it was an accident?"

"Yes, that was what he said, and he was there and I wasn't. I made him the captain of my guard after those few who were still loyal to my father had left Tiryns. That was the second thing I did after I became king."

"What was the first?"

"You can't guess? I ordered that the pillars of the great hall should be painted blue."

It was mid-morning before we left the ruined manor. Thyestes' men had been driven back almost beyond the borders of Tiryns and Argos; almost but not quite. They held a slope of olives that grew above the place where the road up

47

the plain forked; north was the way to Corinth, to the east Mycenae. They were just on our land and seemed content to come no further. Scouts had reported camps being made round the cisterns in the middle of the orchards. The larger part of our combined armies remained to guard the frontier, but the two kings returned to Argos, the nearer of the two citadels.

They rode together in one chariot. I watched them, over the tossing heads of my own team, as Diomedes flicked the whip above the shoulders of his horses and turned them towards home. I followed, with their dust in my throat and stinging my eyes, and I knew that it was more than the sleepless nights that had made me feel tired when I saw the power their youth still gave them to see the sky suddenly clear again because the sun comes out from behind one cloud.

I was jealous. On the night when we had ridden together to Argos I had thought that Diomedes would need me now in a new way; that there would be times in the new complexity of life in a palace when he would be glad of the comfort and guidance I could still give him. I understood now that I had been thinking as a woman thinks, of how a word said in the evening, or early before the day, might guide Diomedes without seeking to control him. It showed me again how different I was from him. I had not wanted the open power that I might have taken by right of my knowledge of the new king and my place in his affection. It was as if I was a man who must live his life always one step away from the centre; as I guided my team it was they who pulled the chariot, as I had taught a prince it was he who ruled; one day I would sit to watch the corn grow at Dimini and it would have been planted for someone else.

Dimini. The track behind the western foothills that hid it from Argos ran up among the corn lands to the right. In a moment I could have swung aside from the column of chariots, and the men marching in the heat, their packs over their spears like country boys going to market. It would be good to be home, and drinking the wine we had pressed ourselves. Then I remembered Diomedes, a laughing half-naked boy, legs splashed purple to the thigh, sucking a wasp-stung hand as we trod the grapes the autumn before. Dimini was his home too; I had not worked myself weary during the days and lain awake at nights planning his good, to leave him now because there was already the man in him that I had hoped he would become. We must be as we were and thinking would not change it.

We reached Argos in the full heat of the early afternoon. A room had been prepared for Leander near the apartments of the king, but I did not think that he would use it except to sleep. They went laughing up the wide main stairway with its tapering pillars, their friendship one of the sudden things that come with early manhood between boys who look for something more exciting than the company of those they have known from childhood, where nothing is forgotten or allowed to change. It might be over as quickly as it had begun but I hoped not, for it is not good to give the heart quickly and then regret the gift.

I followed them slowly towards Diomedes' sleeping room, carrying his helmet and shield. Already the servants bowing in the hall and the guard at the door seemed familiar, and I was ready to laugh at my thought of the morning even before Diomedes turned to see that the door was closed and then sat down suddenly, tired now that the excitement of arrival was over.

"Hipponax, what do you think happens now?"

I poured wine for Leander, and took it to him where he stood looking from the window at the horses being led back through the great gateway of the palace and round to the stable yard.

49

"I expect that before you're clean from the dust of the road my brother will be bowing in the doorway to ask when the Council of Leaders is to be called."

"And before evening there will surely be word from Thyestes," added Leander. "Even though our men and his have sat down to watch each other like two packs of hounds that are thinking better of fighting now they have some blood to lick off, we still don't know why he attacked. When we do we can plan. We should sleep now, Diomedes, it's too hot to think of anything sensible."

I heard the clanking of the guard coming to attention outside and went to the door. Damon had only stopped to change his cloak and rub the worst of the dust from his armour.

Diomedes' mouth twitched as he got up from the bed. "Damon, have we a full account of our losses yet, men and chariots?"

"It should be ready by dusk, my lord. The last of the hundreds is still coming up through the town and all the captains haven't reported yet."

"Very well, summon the captains to the great hall when the lists are ready; we can work as we eat, and there may be news from Mycenae by then."

"Yes, my lord." Damon bowed and went out, bending his head as his helmet plumes touched the lintel, but he gripped my arm as he went and I knew that later he would want to talk to me.

Diomedes had sat down again and was unfastening his belt. "What shall we say to them tonight, Leander?"

"I found it was useful when I was newly king to ask first for the reports of my captains; then I could twist what they had told me into one strand, and it came out like my own opinion. You might try it yourself."

"The wisdom of Tiryns! Leander, this invasion of Thyestes,

it's bigger than any of the small border squabbles that happened when my grandfather was king."

"Yes, it is."

"I never thought Argos could change, with a High King in Mycenae, and us all holding land from him and so on down the line to the swine-herd at Dimini with his two acres of barley. Now already things are different and won't ever be quite as they were before."

"High Kings have always come and gone, and the pattern has changed a little with each of them," said Leander.

"But is the whole framework breaking up now, will Mycenae be just one kingdom? Do you think he's strong enough to do that?"

"He may believe he is. You don't know yet, Diomedes. Being a king isn't like anything else. There is a power that goes out through a king to his people, and being the channel which this power uses will change a man, any man. If it's good to be a king at all, then it must be better to be a greater king; I've thought it myself during the last year, as you have cause to know."

"Not any longer, Leander?"

"No, those are thoughts that come when one is too much alone." Diomedes put his dagger down and Leander picked it up.

"This is fine work."

"It was my father's, he had it before he came to Argos."

Leander drew his own. I was silent, although I had not known till then that metal could be made into something so perfect, but Diomedes drew in his breath and his hand went out almost against his will to touch the lovely thing. It was bronze, beautifully balanced and with a pommel of chased gold, yet it was the blade that held the eye. Down the centre ran a band scarcely more than a finger's-width of dark enamel. Inlaid into it were little men of gold in clothes of silver who

51

fought against a pride of lions snarling from among silver lilies, though each was no bigger than a hornet. Leander turned the dagger and I saw that on the back there were no men, only more lions, and that side was almost the more beautiful. Leander put it into Diomedes' hands.

"It's very old," he said. "Even older than your helmet. No man alive even in Crete could make such work now, but the blade keeps its edge."

"Can there be another as beautiful anywhere?" asked Diomedes.

"In Mycenae perhaps. They have whole swords of this work there. Diomedes, will you take it from me and give me yours, as a pledge between us?"

Diomedes' hands trembled. There was a moment of complete silence that lasted as he looked into the level, grey eyes of the king of Tiryns like an awestruck child who cannot believe that his dearest wish has come true. Then he laid the dagger down and put his own into Leander's outstretched hands.

"Let it be for a sign that the swords of Argos and Tiryns are only drawn to protect each other or in the same cause." Then, a boy again, "Leander, do you really mean it?"

"Of course!" Leander laughed. "Your blade is as good to kill an enemy as mine, and it's meant as much to you in the past."

Diomedes' face split into an enormous grin as he slid the dagger into his own sheath. With his hand still curled round the pommel he said, "Now I can face a council of the captains of Argos. Leander, you have a lion name, and now I carry lions; I wonder if they will prove as strong as the Standing Lions over the great gate of Mycenae."

5

CAPTAINS IN COUNCIL

THE lords of Argos were hungry and there was little conversation as the maids passed from one to the other with the steaming bowls of meat. I set down the tall wine jug and looked through the golden haze of the lamps to the patch of velvet darkness above the ramparts that was framed by the great door. It was a night without stars and the moon was still low. The fire on the central hearth had sunk to glowing ashes, no more than a thread of smoke to drug the midges that whined in the still summer night. Above the small circle of men the high roof had gathered the shadows among the weaving of its great beams. It was a feasting quite different from the last the king had made.

Diomedes had come down from his high seat to eat with the other men, sitting at one table with Leander. They had drunk little, knowing how wine would cloud minds already dulled with sleeplessness. No one seemed anxious to begin the council.

Then I saw Leander look up at the galleries that circled three sides of the hall, and bend to speak to Diomedes.

He put down his wine cup and sat back in his chair. "Damon, is the guard set? And up there?"

At my brother's order I saw the gleam of bronze show for a moment at the head of the great stairway.

"My lords, to business." There was a shuffle and a faint clinking of men settling themselves in more attentive positions, but before Diomedes could proceed the guard outside clattered to attention, there was a glittering of gold and the colours of a peacock in the doorway and a breath of perfume, heavy and dark in the still air above the smells of cooling meat and wine.

"My Lady Persea," said Diomedes, rising slowly to his feet. "Do you join us in our council?"

The tiny painted figure did not speak. She paused while the startled squires hurried forward to move her carved chair. When it had been set down across the hearth from where the two kings sat, she made a small movement with her hand, dismissing her attendants, and sailed across the floor with the same soft tinkling of her gilded skirts, and again a heavy wafting of perfumes from the oil that glistened on the dark ringlets piled beneath the jewelled flowers of her crown.

I saw Diomedes look down at Leander, and the slight gesture palm upwards that he made to him. "So be it. May the Mistress, through her priestess, bless our councils." He sat down again, his right hand fingering the pommel of the lion dagger.

"Achates," said Leander. "Have you the reports I asked for from across the river?" He turned to Diomedes. "It seemed to me that as your guest it would be my duty to give some account of what strength I could bring to the confederacy."

Achates turned to his squire and took from him two clay tablets; for a moment his head, the dark hair already threaded with grey, was bent over the columns of figures, then he looked up.

"As you will already know, my lords, the fighting of the last days has been mostly on this side of the river, although the High King's first attack was launched against both the kingdoms. After we had brought our main strength northward he withdrew all but a few skirmishers so that he might push south through Argos. Our patrols will give warning of any further threat along our eastern frontier, but I think that we can expect that when the battle is joined again it will not be in Tiryns."

Then followed the careful lists of figures, killed, wounded men, broken chariots, farms destroyed, cattle driven north; and with them the other side of the balance, swords and spears, corn enough for two armies, eight hundreds of men already under arms, besides those who now guarded the frontier.

Kaletor followed, speaking for Argos; when both of them had finished there was a long silence.

"And Thyestes?" asked Leander at last, sitting back and grasping the arms of his chair.

Achates made a shape with his hands that seemed to take in the combined strength of the two kingdoms, and then drew them apart toppling with the power of Mycenae.

"If we knew why! Why this attack came and then why it slackened." Diomedes' voice was altered with uncertainty.

Damon looked towards the doorway where one of his captains had just appeared, raising his spear in a signal. "The answer to that would appear to have come at your word, Lord King," he said. "A messenger from Mycenae is even now entering the lower courtyard."

There was a scraping of stools, the squires came forward to take away the last of the wine cups, Diomedes settled the folds of his cloak. Then in the silence the clatter of chariot wheels could be heard, the words of command passed back from the captain of the guard, the tramp of feet.

As the messenger of Thyestes entered the hall there was a hiss, quickly silenced, of shocked surprise. This was not the herald of Mycenae with his white staff of office. The High King had sent his Cretan. In all Mycenae there was only one man who served Thyestes by his own choice; coming as he did from across the sea he owed the king no bond of loyalty,

55

no homage for land, no fear. What had brought him to the
court of Mycenae no man knew, nor all the ways he served the
king, part cupbearer, part captain. It might be that something
cold and power-seeking in the mind of Thyestes had called to

his own nature, and now he was the eyes to observe, and the noiseless footsteps to track down, that uneasy nobles of Mycenae knew in their dreams.

A sense of outrage, thick like mist, rose in the hall as the silence lengthened, and the man who now stood before the two kings turned his head so that his slow inspection seemed to cover every detail of the great hall as he stood swaying a little, one hand on his hip.

Now as his own glance fastened on Diomedes, every eye in the hall was on him, and he knew and desired it. He was of medium height and slightly built, clean shaven, his long curls twined with golden chains like a girl's. He followed the Cretan custom in his clothing, or lack of it, for his body was bare except for a short azure kilt and a dazzle of jewels. Every detail of his appearance, from the long ear-rings, the tight-drawn belt to the gilded leather boots, was feminine in its delicate opulence, yet a hard raw toughness seemed to pulse from him with the strength and lack of subtlety of the Lady Persea's perfume.

The silence began to have the texture of something that can be touched and smelled; Achates coughed, and the great hall seemed to echo. Then the Cretan's right boot tapped, once, twice on the painted floor. He swung round and stepped back so that he was addressing the whole council.

"This is the word of Thyestes, High King of Mycenae, to the lords of Argos and Tiryns." The voice was loud, metallic. "For too long the house of Atreus has watched while the men of the two kingdoms were ruled first by princelings grown childish, and now indeed by children. Such kings are only fit to be cut down as the corn that grows, not for the ruling of men. If the land is to return to the old pattern it shall be because the High King wills it and in no other way. Let the men of Argos choose if they will be ruled any longer by boys."

Achates was on his feet, the angry rumble of a stream about

57

to burst its banks came from the other men. Leander's hand stayed them as he sat beside a Diomedes who seemed suddenly frozen, his face blanched with weariness.

"Now hear the second word of the king," cried the Cretan. "Let the men of Argos know that the roofs remain unburned above their heads and their cattle unslaughtered only because I stay my hand. The moon is already four days past the full; when it rises new again over the eastern mountains I will take the land in blood if by then the lords of Argos have not brought me the earth and water of submission."

Even as the last words rang between the pillars he turned, not waiting for a reply, and strode out into the pearl-touched shadows of the rising moon.

Two heartbeats after the last sound of his footsteps had died away the shouting began. Diomedes strode to the centre of the group beside the hearth, the furious blood rising back into his face and staining his bare neck and throat. I had never seen him so angry.

"Men of Argos!" It was the Diomedes of the loud war-cry. "We are your kings by birth and by the labour of the Gods, not by our own choice. Will you have us as we are, to live and die for you—with you? Or shall it be as Thyestes boasts? Did we prove ourselves to be children when our lands were attacked, did we fight only in play?"

He turned away, one hand groped towards the pillar, and I knew that he was battling with tears of weariness and injustice, yet there was no way that I could reach him across the hall. It was Kaletor who rose to his feet and laid a great arm matted with dark hair across the boy's shoulders, turning him back to his seat. He pushed him back into it with almost the shake of an exasperated mother.

"You are our leader, little King, never fear. Maybe that mountebank was sleeping when you led the men who cleared the south road two days ago, and those who stay for no answer deserve none. Let us be calm now and think what must be done and who there is to do it."

He did not go back to his place, standing protectively on the left side of the king. I could not see Diomedes' face as I stood behind him, but his shoulders still heaved as if his breath was coming hard.

The other men of the council were back in their seats by now, yet the stale weariness that had hung in the hall before the message of the Cretan had gone. Only the Lady Persea sat on, seemingly unmoved, her colour unchanging under the paint that masked her face.

"Ten days," said Leander. "Ten days to gather our forces and seek for new allies before we fight for our lives. Thyestes shows a strange generosity, or perhaps he is only playing with us, like a child who has a bird tied by one leg."

"My lords, King Leander is right, this is hard to understand." It was Damon who was speaking now, in a grave, puzzled voice. "We still have no answer to the strange pattern of the fighting. First the High King attacks, then his men withdraw; the last days have been more like clearing the cattle out of a cornfield than driving back a determined enemy. Now he even sends word of the day when he will fight again, as if this was a tournament. Can he be so sure already that no help can come to us? How can we know what we must do until we can understand this much?"

"How? Perhaps the Gods will show us that, for understand we must." Achates leaned forward. "Damon, this will perhaps be part of the High King's plan, to conquer us by confusion."

Diomedes asked in a strange husky voice, "There are kings in Corinth and Nemea, will they fight for Thyestes or against him?"

"There has been no love lost between Argos and Nemea since the days of your father, King Diomedes," said Mecistheos. "There will be no help from there, and the men of Corinth and Troizen must fight their way through passes held by Mycenae to come to us."

Then Achates, the bowman, threw back his head with the laugh of a man who sees the simple answer to a problem he thought impossible to solve. He stood up, a thickset man with a face that seemed always to be contradicting itself, part grim, part gentle. When he spoke I realized that I had not heard before how his flexible voice, the instrument of the musician he also was, could make a picture in his hearers' minds that was far beyond that of his words alone.

"My lords, now we are indeed about the game that Thyestes began among us. He will be watching us, these days, while we try one way of escape after another, like foxes whose earths have been stopped. He will intercept our messages, cut off all attempts to help us, and then when the time comes he will pounce. But there is one direction from which help may yet come. Remember Sparta, my lords, and Agamemnon."

"What could he do? If he had men enough of his own he would have taken Mycenae long ago; it's his by right, he's the eldest son of his father. Thyestes is his uncle, with no true claim to the kingdom," said Diomedes.

"Yes," said Achates. "Yet before he would have been one man alone, with whatever men his wife's father, the king of Sparta, would give him. In former days the kings of Argos and Tiryns would not have helped him. Why should they risk their own thrones? Now in one moment the armies of the two kingdoms are behind him, and there will surely be men in Mycenae itself who are glad of a chance to change kings. Thyestes is not a man to care if his subjects love him, and by all accounts Agamemnon is a gallant soldier."

"Kaletor, could our messenger reach Sparta in time for Agamemnon to gather his forces and be here before the new moon?" asked Diomedes, turning in his chair.

Kaletor counted it out on his thick fingers. "Two, perhaps three days for a chariot to get through the mountains. Twice as long for foot soldiers. The time would be very short."

"But it would be possible?" urged Diomedes.

"Yes, if Agamemnon is at home, and swift to make decisions."

"Then we must pray to the Mistress he is both. My lords, there is nothing more for the moment that we can do. The fate of both our kingdoms, and the name of the man who will be High King when the moon is full again, rests with Agamemnon, and those we send to him as emissaries." He turned to Leander. "If the Lord Achates would go, we in Argos would rest more easily."

Achates dropped to one knee before the two young men. "If my king wills it, only let me have a captain of Argos to go with me."

As the two kings left the hall the lords stood, and the Lady Persea also rose to her feet. With a bow to the company that was so slight that the lilies of her head-dress hardly trembled, she glided out of the door. She had not spoken one word.

As I turned to follow Diomedes, Damon caught me by the arm. "Come to my quarters when the king is asleep. It seems to me that this council has asked more questions than it has answered."

6

VOICES IN THE NIGHT

At last Leander had gone along the painted passage to his own room and I helped the servants to put Diomedes to bed. He was so weary that we could scarcely keep him awake long enough to dress the wound in his neck. For the moment the hours of most urgent strain were over; the morning and the days beyond it would bring troubles enough, but he was young and this was the first time for four nights that he had slept in a bed.

It was dark and very hot in the sleeping room as I bathed my own face and arms and then threw myself down still fully dressed to wait till Diomedes was really asleep. The little flame flickered beside my bed in the last of the lamps left burning, and a mosquito droned unpleasantly in my ear.

Diomedes made a humphing sound and burrowed deeper into the goose feather mattress. I stood up and reached for my cloak, hearing the dragging out of his long slow breaths. The door opened silently and I hushed the guard until I had it closed behind me.

"I won't be gone more than half an hour. If the king wakes, send for me to the quarters of the captain of the guard."

Damon looked up from the wine cup he held in both hands as I greeted him. He was sitting as I had so often seen him, long legs stretched far out, his head forward, thinking as if all the power of his deliberation was in his twisted lower lip.

"Hipponax, I feel like a fly in a spider's web," he said.

"Every time I pull one leg free the other gets stuck somewhere else."

I didn't answer him straight away, looking round me at the room he now occupied with its frieze of warriors and the armour hanging on pegs in the wall. Then I said, "What is it, Damon? What's bothering you worst of all? I remember when you were a boy you could never really deal with more than one thing at a time; funny that you're the one with red hair!"

"Couldn't I? I suppose not, but at least I concentrated on whatever it was that I was doing!"

That made me laugh. It had always been like that. Damon was a year younger than I and yet his power of excelling at whatever was important to him at the time had given him a directness which often carried him beyond me. One by one he had mastered the skills every man must learn and now he sat in the room of the captain of the guard while I was nothing more than a favoured servant.

"Do you know how things have shapes?" asked Damon, his red head bending over the clasped hands again. "You can feel if they're right or not, even if it's the way things happen and not the way they look that's important. These last days have been all wrong, it's all happening too neatly or not neatly enough. As if there's one mind behind it all, and that not a nice one."

"Whose could it be? Thyestes? No, how could he have made the old king ill?"

"No, not Thyestes. At least, I don't know, perhaps not directly. Think back a few months. Argos has a king with a son to follow him; first this son who is still a child is away from home, staying with kinfolk, and because of his age more likely than not to be murdered on the journey even if he was sent for to come home.

"Then the old sickness that has affected the king in the past comes back, and worse than before. On one day he runs mad, a day when his new heir is there close by in the hills, an heir who is not strong enough to be a threat and yet not so weak a child that he will be set aside. Now who, Hipponax, could do all this and then have it that Leander and his Tirynians were already at our borders and Thyestes poised to strike? And who could draw back the armies in just this way so that we have hope and yet no grounds for a real faith in it?"

"I don't know, Damon, all those questions are just words without answers. I suppose that same mind, if there is one, has made it so that we've been too busy from hour to hour to think clearly what we are doing. Yet what else could we have done? Diomedes was next in line to be king, and surely he's done as well and better than anyone could hope for?"

I was waiting like a mother, for her child to be praised. "Has he?" asked Damon, looking up at me for the first time. "Yes, perhaps he has, all we could have hoped for from a boy." The way he said it made the word sound very young.

"Damon, he's fought and marched and watched with us all these days. He's made decisions quickly that a man would have hesitated at."

"Perhaps the man would have been right. No, sit down, Hipponax, I'm not criticising your nurseling, not really. It's just that the one thing Diomedes cannot change is his age. It is not possible for a boy, any boy, to know all that should be known by a king. A boy may shout and charge, a king must know when to draw back, and how to wait and yet hold his men quiet and steady behind him. Leander, I think, could do it, and the training that has made it possible in him so young has stunted other things that will never grow now."

There was no answer to that. I drooped in the chair beside my brother, so weary now that even the walk back along the darkened passages to the king's room seemed beyond me. The minutes were passing and Diomedes might wake, and now with Damon's careful words sifting the hope from my mind I did not know what I would find to say to comfort him. It was after midnight and it seemed as if the weakening moon was drawing all my future into its death.

"So you see how it is," said Damon with his rare and delightful smile, "how it is that I'm confused. There is this shape in my mind all the time of the brain that could think all this plan and make it happen, and while I'm seeking after that like a child hunting for a voice in a game of blindfold, I am watching Diomedes and praying to the Mistress that if she ever made a king and made one quickly she will do it again."

"And all this while some brain that isn't your own is giving orders to the guard and behaving as a king's captain should."

"Am I? I hoped I was. As you say, there hasn't been time to notice. But, Hipponax, my new duties are far easier than yours."

That made me gasp. "What duties?"

"Don't you see, that's just the point. I know more or less what's expected of me; the first time you hold a watch, or even march four men the way you want them to go and not into a wall, that's the difficult time. After that it's only the same but bigger. No, I know who you are, what you see you must do; does anyone else except yourself? Not Diomedes, Leander perhaps, and yet you will be as important in Argos in these days ahead as any one of us, perhaps more than any."

"But Diomedes. . . ."

"Yes, because of your Diomedes! Already he isn't the same, is he? He has changed as the sun changes from hour to hour, and so you have been marking him as a wrestler does his partner. Somewhere there will be a word, or a weakness; you must see it and be ready. I don't know, I feel strange tonight, as if there were a god in my head thinking thoughts I can't understand. I'm seeing everything from very high up. It's as if the next few days and the battle at the end of them are not

65

nearly as important as ourselves and the people round us, and who we really are."

I stood up. "Do you think sleep would make your thoughts man-size again, Damon? I've never known you like this and you scare me silly. The worst thing is that I know you're right and I've known it all along. The Mistress grant that whatever happens I can keep at least in speaking distance of Diomedes, so he'll listen. . . ."

There was a scratching at the door. "The king, sir," said the young guard. "Will you come, we think he's talking in his sleep."

Damon's hand on my shoulder sent me out of the room a little comforted. As I hurried to the king's room, I pushed all that he had said deeper into my tired mind, now that I had a practical thing to deal with and one that was not altogether unexpected.

The door of the room stood a little ajar. "It's quiet again now, sir," said the other guard. "But I thought I'd better be sure."

"It's time I was resting, anyway, " I said, and slid the door to behind me.

I sat down on my bed and watched the sleeping boy. He was restless; first an arm thrown out, then a muttered word. For a while he seemed to sleep more quietly, and my head was nodding forward as my eyes tired, staring at the frieze of dolphins that seemed to swim in a tossing sea as the beginning of the night wind sent the shadows of the curtains dancing across them.

Diomedes muttered again, gasped and sat up, then before I could reach him he was out of bed and tearing at the curtains, sobbing and calling my name.

I reached him before he got them down and tried to pull him back towards the bed. It was only then that I saw he was still asleep, eyes tightly closed, lost in some private and terrible

66

world of his own. The bedcover was still caught round his legs; I pulled it free and put it round him, for he had begun to tremble. Then I took him by the shoulders, shaking him gently to bring him to himself.

It seemed a long time before he sagged back on the bed and opened his eyes, stickily, like a baby. I sat down, my arm still round his shoulders.

He peered through the wavering light. "Oh, Hipponax, you're here," and he buried his head against my shoulder.

"Was it a dream?" I asked.

"A dream? I suppose so, but I haven't dreamed like that since I was a child." Again a fit of trembling shook him.

"Tell me what it was."

The words came in broken sentences as he tried to give names to the enormous shapes that still swirled in his mind.

"I think I was in a wood, it was dark and wet—the branches seemed wet, they caught in my hair. I don't know where I was going, but I was frightened and I didn't want to go. . . . Then the branches pulled my tunic off and still I had to go on. I think there were people but they were mixed up with the trees, I couldn't see them, but they were there, and there was something I had to go to. Then I reached it. It was like a great rock, I was flat against it at the bottom, and I looked up through the dark, but I could see the rock and it went back further than anything, taller than a mountain—and I had to climb it. I can feel the stone. . . ."

He broke off and sniffed hard, his hands feeling in front of him as if he was still trying to cling to the rock.

"I climbed on and on, it seemed as if it was for years, and there were still branches pulling at me, and then they weren't branches. It was like the flounces on a woman's dress and I was climbing up, like a tiny wet ant, fighting my way through them. Then I was near the top and I could see the woman. I

67

don't know where I was standing because I could see all of her, and she was big as a mountain, only her face was wrong, it was like a man's, like I've imagined Thyestes. He looked at me and I wasn't only naked, it was as if there was no skin on me and he was looking through to my bones. He had an axe. I saw it in his, no, her hand and it was tiny, a child's axe, only it grew and grew. And she held it over me and said 'Be my husband, or I'll kill you,' and I said 'I can't, I'm too small,' and she laughed and the axe kept on growing. . . .''

He stopped and I put my arms round him and comforted him as well as I could, but I was frightened myself now. This was no ordinary dream, there were things in it that I did not think Diomedes could know about waking, and I hoped he would not remember them again when morning came.

I was a man, but I was of the soil of Argos in a way he could never be, and I feared Potnia, the Mother, mistress of the wild things. I had heard of the time when a man had been a thing without power before the women of his house, and Argos was ruled by a queen. There had been no marriage then as we knew it and the queen would mate as she chose so that as she was fertile the harvest might be also, and each spring a new young king would be cut down so that corn would sprout in the earth that held his body. There had been a dark memory of this in the message of Thyestes.

This had been the old way, but it had changed and the very memory of it had weakened in our minds as we became over the generations a mingled people. Now the Horse King of the warriors was the god a man with a brazen sword would cry to as he rode to battle. And yet while the men ride out the women, waving from the house doors, remain at home, and the mysteries of women alter more slowly, circling as they do about the things that are never different, birth and dying and the flowing of life between. Could this dream of Diomedes have come from a woman and from the power behind women?

68

From the Lady Persea? I could see no way of finding an answer to that, or of learning how far her power ran.

Diomedes grew quiet. I helped him to bathe his face and gave him a sweet drink to sip while I remade the disordered bed. Then I lit another lamp so that there were no shadows, and sat beside him until he slept again. I did not think that the dream could come again that night.

When I lay down at last on my own bed I was so tired that even its unfamiliar comfort could not bring my body rest immediately. The moon sent a silver finger over the window sill and it was cooler, so I pulled the bedcover up over my shoulders. Who in Argos could help me now, I wondered, as the weight of what I had been told and what I now knew for myself, lay upon my heart.

7

WOMEN OF ARGOS

PHILON came to me very early in the morning, before the palace was fully awake, as I stood in the coolness of the first hour after sunrise looking out over the great courtyard from the balcony at the end of the upper passage. The sick taste of not enough sleep was still in my mouth and my head was thick with the beginnings of a headache. The second cock crow had woken me and I was both cursing my own wakefulness and blessing the capacity of the young to sleep through anything.

When he tugged at the corner of my tunic, I had to think hard to remember when I had seen this thin, small boy before.

"Philon, what is it?"

"Will the king wake up if you don't go back at once?" he asked.

"No, not for a while yet, did you want me?"

"Yes. No, not me exactly, someone else does, only it's very private."

"Who is it?"

"Will you come now without me telling you? I said I wouldn't." He looked solemn but unexpectedly confident, so different from the distraught child of a few days before that I saw at once someone must have been looking after him; even his tunic was cleaner and newly patched.

"All right, if it isn't far. I mustn't be gone long."

"Don't come at once or people will see us together. I'll go

down first, and when you see from up here which way I go you can follow me."

He darted away before I could ask him any more questions, although by now the whole idea was beginning to sound more like a child's game than anything else. I could not imagine what danger there could be in my walking openly through the citadel with a child like Philon. However, before I had time to change my mind he had re-appeared below me, running out into the sunlight in the direction of the stairway that led to the lower courtyard.

I followed more slowly, down through the great hall, across both courtyards, down stairways and finally under the pointed arch that led to the oldest levels of the citadel. Here we were almost in the rock itself, in a place where small storage rooms were built into the thickness of the outer walls. It was dark, stuffy and smelled strongly of cedar wood and spice, for some of the richest treasures of Argos were here.

Light flickered on the lintel of a half-open door at the end of the passage. Philon was nowhere to be seen. The guards were all above in the sunlight and it was very quiet. I don't know who I thought would be waiting in the little room, but it wasn't my cousin Chryseis. She was kneeling on the floor beside an open chest, staring at the doorway and obviously terrified. If it had not been for that first evening in the great hall, I'm not sure that I would have known her because now that we were face to face I could see just how subtly the year at court had altered her. The hair and style of dress were new of course, and she was changed from the child at Dimini to the maid of a princess; girls can make these alterations with a swiftness that is baffling to men. What I saw now was something outside this, a watchfulness that was not simply the greater control that maturity brings, something restless and unhappy hidden behind the eyes. Yes, it was mostly her eyes that were different.

71

Chryseis stood up, shaking out her skirts. "You've grown," I said, stupidly.

"It was time I did!" I remembered then that she had always been the smallest of the girls at Dimini.

"Philon," she said. "Keep watch." The child squatted down in the doorway where he could see down the passage.

Chryseis shut the lid of the chest and sat down on it. "Hipponax, I thought after the king's feast that I could see you and ask you all the things I want to know about Dimini. It's so near and I'm silly to miss it so much, but you know how it is. Then there was the fighting and I realized that now I might not ever speak to you again."

For a moment my eyes left her and strayed round the low tunnel-roofed room with its chests and jars.

"I know what you're thinking. Why bring you down here to ask about my sister's baby, but that's not important now. Oh Hipponax, I'm so frightened."

Suddenly her whole face seemed to have slipped, the restlessness behind her eyes had the loosened rootless look of terror. Who more than I could recognize it, since I had lived the last days in the same state? I sat down on the chest beside her, near enough to take one of the hands that was pleating and twisting at her skirt.

"What is it, Chryseis? Something new, or something that's gone on so long that you can't bear it any more?"

"Both really. Listen, I don't know how long we can talk, let me tell you the important thing first. It's a message for the king."

"Diomedes?"

"Yes, you are his cupbearer, aren't you? He listens to you?"

"In a way, yes, but . . ."

"Hipponax, let me tell you if I can. It's difficult because it's the sort of message you would usually think was just women's talk and not take any notice of."

"Who sent it?"

"A woman. No, you've never met her, but she risked a nasty death to speak to me."

"Can you tell me who she is?"

"Slowly! I have to think of my words because you're a man and this is all part of the things I shouldn't speak about to you. You know I serve the Lady Persea and that she's the priestess of the Mistress. Usually when the ceremonies have to be performed, we go to the grove below the town, near the river. Some of the things that happen there everyone knows about, like the times when the king comes. But there are other things, things that happen at night . . ."

Her words were weaving a picture in my mind. I could see the deep shadow of the trees and smell the perfume and the excitement of the waiting women. I had been holding her hand in the comforting way that one does with a child; now her fingers twisted and gripped mine more tightly. Her voice was soft and very quick.

"I don't know everything my lady does there, and I don't want to, I'm not an initiate, but some of the women in the town are. One is a woman they call Latromis the harlot, I don't know her real name. She has a little house below the wall of the citadel; she was there before I came to the palace."

"How do you know her?"

"Through a mistake. I remember it was when the priestess had been down at the grove all night, and at dawn I was sent with a message. I was going to knock at the side gate in the wall that leads into the main precinct when the little door opened and Latromis came out. She looked terrible, breathing like someone who's been beaten almost senseless—and there were great bruises on her arms. At first she didn't see me because she had swayed back against the wall as if she couldn't stand upright any more, and her hair was loose over her face. Hipponax, I knew what she was but there wasn't anything else

73

a woman could have done, I went to her and helped her home. We didn't talk at all, even when she got to the door of her house, but she looked at me once as if she was grateful. The next day in the market a man put a packet into my hands; it was these ear-rings." She moved her head to show me the gold flowers that danced on their fine chains. "I don't know why she was so grateful, it was such a little thing to do."

"It was this Latromis who sent you the message?"

"Yes, only she came herself. There's a way into the palace at night, but I daren't tell even you where it is. This is what she said. 'Let the king remember that there are women beyond Argos who serve the Mistress, and their loyalty may be wider than their menfolk would understand. In the old days a woman's voice was important in council, now most are silent, but even when their lips are closed their ears are open.' "

"Is she warning us of something inside the palace?" I asked.

"I don't know, she wouldn't say any more, not that I can tell you; but she was very frightened. Diomedes must be on his guard to see that what he plans to do is known by as few people as possible even within the palace. Not only the big things but the small details that will be important in the next attack. I didn't understand all she said, but Latromis seemed to be afraid that some power was loose that was more terrible than we understand even yet, something more difficult to stop than Thyestes' army. You will tell Diomedes, won't you?"

"Yes, I suppose I must, but it's hard to know how. This is uncanny stuff for a man to talk about, and he's already frightened enough." I told her about Diomedes' dream, and then—surprised myself that already I was trusting her so implicitly—what Damon had said to me the evening before.

She stood up then and paced as far as the doorway where the child still sat watchfully, his eyes on the passage outside. Then she knelt down in front of me so that her face was on a level with mine.

"No, I was wrong, it's too late; don't tell him anything. It may be that the power he has because he's the king will be strong enough on its own to save him. You understand, don't you, now, where the danger is?"

"Chryseis, we can't be fighting the Gods!"

"No," she said in a small, tired voice. "But it seems there are people who would like to make us think so; I think the truth is much simpler than that."

"I must get you safely out of the palace, Chryseis."

"Stop thinking like a relation, Hipponax; we both serve the king and our country is at war. There may be some doings in the palace you can only have news of from me, and only then if I can stay here unprotected, that's why I asked you to meet me here. Philon can bring my messages."

The boy looked up at the sound of his name and smiled at her. It was very clear now who had mended the tears in his tunic.

As I looked at the small, slim, brown-haired girl in front of me, with her warm eyes, I began to realize how a mother must feel when she sends her son away into danger for the first time, only this danger she must live with was a silent faceless one that must be fought with a flawless mask of innocence, and quite alone.

She stood up and touched me gently on the shoulder, and I knew that my face had been betraying my thoughts, because she said, "You used not to worry like a mother hen. Is it Diomedes? Is he all right, really all right? He will make a king, won't he? It's hard to imagine it, because when I think of him I always remember the time he fell out of the hay rick and I laughed. When I saw him in the hall in all his robes it seemed only another children's game."

"He's all right," I said, standing up so that she need not see my face. "Yes really, and now there's Leander. I must go, when shall we meet again?"

"Don't plan anything, I'll send when there's news, and you can too. I'll make sure that Philon is about the palace when he's needed."

As I walked back down the passage I knew two things. The first was the very simple one that for the first time it mattered that I should be in my cousin's company, and I was sad to leave her; the second one was that if we both came safely to the new moon no power that she could use would stop me taking her home to the friendliness and simplicity of Dimini. And so I came back to the king's chambers and there was still no one person to whom I could tell all that was in my mind.

It was strange that it was now in this pause in the middle of of war that Diomedes began to learn for the first time what is the hardest thing about being a king. Achates was already deep into the mountains in the southwest, on the road to Sparta, but in the citadel there was much to be done. One by one the palace officials came to the great hall to give an account of their services, and the wealth and strength that Argos could summon up for the great struggle that lay ahead. It was not only the tally of men and chariots and horses. The scribes, fresh from the great storerooms, stood with their clay tablets; so many leather helmets, so many swords of bronze, spear heads, shafts in bundles, some ready mounted, some not.

Then the treasurer began. Wine and corn to supply the army, wagons to carry it; twenty smiths from the western manors who must come to help the palace armourers, men who owed service to their lords who could be sent south to the harbour to unload hides from Thessaly. None of this was strange to Leander; he stood on one side of the king's seat, playing with a hound, and steered Diomedes' course among the demands of prudence and necessity, till the new entries were scratched into the wet clay and sealed with the king's seal, and all that could be made ready was at least begun.

In the early evening we stood on the wall above the gate-house which faced to the north. The place where the men of Mycenae were camped under the olive trees was lost in the gentle swelling and falling of the plain, but the sickle of mountains that ran west to east were a clear amethyst in the evening light.

Diomedes said, "I'd rather live through ten days of battle than another one like today."

"You'll learn, Diomedes," said Leander. "It's hard mainly because it's strange. By the winter you'll know most of what you were told today without thinking about it; where the cattle come from for the palace sacrifice, what payment Gelanor must make for his father's manor. It all fits together."

"I must learn to be patient too, Leander. What are we to do now? Nine days till the moon is new. Perhaps three days from now we can begin to hope for a message from Sparta, even if the actual help can't come for much longer than that.

Till then must we watch Mycenae while Mycenae watches us?"

"No, I've been thinking. Thyestes may know by now that we've sent messengers to Sparta; I hope not, but no secret that's known to many people can be kept for ever. Still, even if he knows that a messenger was sent west he may not be sure who we sent him to, and I'm hoping that we can keep him from thinking too much about it."

Diomedes looked across at his friend and began to smile slowly. "Leander, what are you planning?"

"Imagine you're Thyestes in his citadel. You believe that our reinforcements will come from the west. What do you expect us to do?"

"Safeguard the road they're to come by."

"Yes, good. Now, how is Thyestes to prevent this? The road to Sparta lies across our land, remember."

"He could try to cut the road even further back. The king of Nemea, north of Argos, is loyal to him, and if he went through his land it would bring him much further west than we should dare to send our men with his main force so near us."

"Could we prevent him?"

"I don't know, but, Leander, if you're right we've got to, though I don't see how. Hipponax?" He turned to me.

"There are only two things we can do, as I see it," I answered. "Either we can challenge Thyestes' force and prevent it ever reaching the western road, or we could make some diversion that would take the High King's mind away from Sparta."

"Which would you choose, Leander, or is there a third way?" asked Diomedes.

"No, Hipponax is right as far as he goes, and so were you, Diomedes. We can't send men back down the road to Sparta, it's too far, and we can't be certain either that Agamemnon

78

will come or Thyestes attack there. If he does Agamemnon must fight his own battle, for we can't send our men north against Nemea either, we have enough enemies of our own already and it would mean fighting our way past Thyestes' men; no, it isn't possible."

"There's one thing we could do," I suggested. "We've no trained men to spare but west in the mountains is my country. Diomedes' father held all the valley of Dimini from the king, and far back into the hills. If we couldn't stop a raiding force at least we could have exact news of it, and my father's shepherds would have their own ways of slowing it down."

"Oh, I wish I wasn't a king, Hipponax! I should love to lie on a mountain side rolling rocks down on Thyestes' chariots."

"You may yet come to it," said Leander with a lopsided grin. "We've seen what we can't do, now we must plan something that's possible. I think we can draw some of Thyestes' forces east of the river. You may know your own mountains, so do I, and I have a country to defend as well as you. This is a time when I think we can make Thyestes' spies work for instead of against us, and not risk too many men. Remember, we may yet have to fight Mycenae alone."

"I do, Leander." Diomedes put his hand on the pommel of the lion dagger. The King of Tiryns saw it and his face lost some of its grimness.

"It's difficult to count men by night. If tomorrow, after dusk, we sent a troop up the main track to Troizen, the king would think either that we were trying to win allies, or that we meant to come round and attack him from behind. Either way he must try to stop us; there are too many paths back through the mountains to Mycenae itself for him to be safe with us there. But the messenger who counted us as we crossed the fords would not be the same man who counted us through the pass to Troizen. All that Thyestes would know would be that we were well into the mountains. So we would be, a quarter of our men, and the rest would have separated from them to wait in ambush not at all where we would be expected. We might not score a great victory over the king's patrols but we should do far more damage than the same number of men could do any other way."

"It would puzzle Thyestes, take a little of the heart from his men, and destroy some of his chariots. And if we stay here like children until we're told that we may attack, we shall certainly be beaten because our men will be afraid. Yes, I see. Leander, it should work, but it must be soon or he'll have time to send his men west. What strength would we need?"

"One hundred men and some chariots as far as the pass. That's enough to make a show, and fight when the time comes, but not so many it would look like a major challenge and loose his whole army after us."

"Us?"

Leander glanced quickly back from studying the distant pass. "I must lead them myself, it's my own country, I know it."

"But 'us', Leander?"

"Your place is here in Argos," I said. "It would be madness for you both to be away together. The plan's a good one, but how if something went wrong and you were both killed together?"

As soon as I'd spoken I knew it had been a foolish thing to say. It was less than a day since the Cretan had called Diomedes a child before the council; since, there had been the long, dull hours of palace business. Now there was a chance to be out riding with his friend, doing something positive against the creeping danger from Mycenae. Damon had warned me, Chryseis had trusted my judgement; now I had said the one thing that would push Diomedes head over heels into foolishness.

He was looking at me with his head back, then he turned to

Leander and said in a strange tight voice, "And does my Lord of Tiryns agree with my cupbearer?"

I felt cold inside and a long way away as Leander said, "Diomedes, there's a lot in what Hipponax says. I must go, you can see that, can't you, but who would you leave in command in Argos?"

"Mecistheos. Leander, do you think I would want to ride with you if I hadn't left my city safe behind me?" He was very haughty now.

"No, of course not, and it would be good to have you fighting with me, don't think I didn't mean that."

I watched them from a few paces away. Diomedes would go with Leander, and I would ride with them, there was no doubt about that, but it was dangerous in a way that I couldn't fully explain even to myself. Leander had been right, an attack of some sort must be made, for it was vital that Thyestes' attention should be turned away from Sparta. We needed a victory, kings and people alike, but must it be with so much to lose if the spies of Thyestes had keener eyes than even Leander supposed?

And I knew more of those spies than the two young men still talking so eagerly. Was this restless impatience that they felt one more of the reasons why Thyestes had granted us ten days' waiting space, knowing that with kings so young such a thing as this must happen? Now by my clumsiness I had spoiled any chance I might ever have possessed of thwarting him even in that.

8

DAWN IN MYCENAE

NEXT day, under cover of the general mobilization, the pre-
parations for the ambush went ahead with the utmost secrecy.
Most of the men who would go were from Tiryns, but some
were our own, and those were picked and would be led by my
brother. I could see from Damon's face when Diomedes told
him of the plan that he was no happier about it than I was,
but there was nothing he or anyone could say now that would
change what had been decided. Outwardly Diomedes was his
old self again with the remoteness of the evening before quite
gone, yet there was an edge of reserve between us as I helped
him to arm that showed itself mainly in a more studied polite-
ness.

Leander came in, wearing the leather corselet of a captain
of one hundred. "No, don't wear your helmet," he said, as
Diomedes picked it up. "It's too well known. No need to
advertise too widely that we're both away together."

I went down the stairs ahead of them to see that the horses
were ready. The Lady Persea had kept to her apartments
more closely than usual during the last day and I had seen
nothing of Chryseis. In a way I was glad, as there was nothing
I could tell her that was in any way hopeful, and the sense of
doom that had been hanging over me ever since the morning
after what had seemed our first victory was clamping down on
to my skull now like a helmet of lead. As there were no wise

words for me to say I could at least see to the stowing of the spears in the chariots.

I ducked out from under the yoke bar in the fading light between the slithering of nervous hooves and nearly fell over Philon, feeding the horses with a twist of hay.

"Chryseis said 'The Mistress go with you'," he said. "But she didn't sound as if she was sure that was a good thing to say."

"How did she know we were going anywhere?" I asked quietly, bending forward to check the buckles on the harness.

"The women know; they always do."

"Do they know where?"

"East."

"Do the men know that too, the ones we're riding with?"

"No, or anyway they were whispering about it in the barracks, asking questions, and no one was giving any answers."

"Philon, stay near Chryseis. It seems as if it's more dangerous being a woman than a man, these days!"

"I will, at least unless I need to be near the king; I promised him first, you see."

Before I could ask him what he meant by that he had slipped out of sight behind the horses. The kings came quietly down to the waiting men, and it was time.

No horns blew as we left the citadel in the fading light. The chariots went slowly in the dust of the marching men, and we were silent; there was the long night ahead and fighting at the end of it for most of us. Diomedes, too, did not speak, but he was restless, peering under the great trees that darkened the road part of the way to the river.

It was night by the time we reached the northern fords where we were to cross. The track broke up into a wide slope of mud, baked hard by the midday sun into a fan of cart ruts. The chariot wheels clattered and slid across them, grating on the large stones at the edge of the river bed. The water had shrunk to a summer trickle, half lost among the tall banks of reeds and the stretches of bleached sand. We splashed through it and up the steep slope beyond; there was only starlight now and a whole army of spies might have lain hidden in the darkness. I was certain that, as we had intended, we had not crossed unseen; but intended or not, no man likes to feel eyes in his back.

We halted a little further on, where the track forked, to let the last of the marchers catch up with us, and Leander pulled in his team alongside. It was too dark to see his face but there was a faint shimmer of white stones on the road ahead and the high line of the pass, a lighter place against the sky.

"The track we're taking strikes north past the next bend in the road. The men have orders to break off up it in twos and threes so that the chariots can go on with no confusion. There may be no one watching, but sound travels at night."

I gave the chariot reins to a waiting groom and dismounted with Diomedes. It seemed strange to be walking behind the horses when the column began to move again. The bend in the road came, a break in the orchards to the left, and a stony path up past terraced vines where we stumbled over the invisible sharp-edged stones, while all the time the sound of the chariots faded below us with the thunder of an army on the march. This would be the first time that I had gone into battle on foot, and as the hours passed the idea lost all the advantages it might ever have seemed to possess. I knew that the sight of my team waiting below in the bright morning light at the appointed place on the Troizen road would be like a second sunrise to me. If they were waiting, and if we were there to see them.

Above the vineyards, higher than the treeline, the rocky hillsides seemed dead and empty, as if no men had ever lived here up on the border between Tiryns and Mycenae. It was after midnight when we came down over the difficult shoulder of the mountain into the valley that Leander had chosen for an ambush. It ran north and south, high and bare, a hillside strewn with great rocks and spiked with scrubby, low ilexes; by day it would be a place where goats and sheep grazed the thin grass; now it was empty of life. We scrambled down what was no more than a cattle track and across the floor of the valley, with its dry stream bed, cut deep into the rock by the winter floods. The pale moon, low in the sky, showed the marks of wheels in the gravel between the dead water plants. This was how the men of Mycenae would come when they had word of Argives so near the citadel.

Leander halted the straggling column and called the captains together. "Here we must separate," he said. "Diomedes, I'll lie up with my men in the rocks above the track. Will you take the lower part of the valley? A little further down it turns eastward round a tower of rock. Wait there and we can take them between us."

Damon asked, "When will that be, my lord?"

"Not till dawn. We've three hours to wait, and if you keep careful watch you may see them before us. I shall wait till they're nearly past before I attack; we should have the advantage of height. Diomedes, get hold of any chariots that break away down the stream bed, if you can, we may need them to get clear."

"What then, Leander?"

"A quick escape. We're too many to hide easily among these bare hills, and too few to fight long in earnest. All we're here to do is to confuse Thyestes and do what damage we can. Take no prisoners unless they look important, and no stopping to strip the dead or capture armour, we can't carry it. When I give the signal we'll make for the south and the main road."

I could tell that Diomedes was uncertain whether or not he was being given a post of greater safety, and that he did not want to leave Leander in this dark, strange valley. As he led the way downhill the land seemed empty under the dying moon, but I could not lose the feeling that eyes were watching us, and our tired feet seemed as noisy as the chariot wheels had been. The round shield bumped and jarred between my shoulders and the blood was thudding in my head so that the very bones of my skull felt heavy and badly fitting.

I stood and waited with the others, tired and lost without my chariot, while Damon set the watch. Then we climbed part of the way up the rock to a place where we could watch the valley and wait for morning. My head was thundering now and my arms ached so that I could hardly pull myself up the last few handholds.

Dawn was not far away and the summer night was cool enough towards the morning for me to be glad of my cloak. I sat hunched up, eyes closed, resting my aching head back against the rock behind me. No one spoke, and I wanted to sleep but I began to realize that the growing discomfort of the last hour was more than the apprehension of a man who has been falling over rocks in the dark for half a night and who is waiting for an attack; I was going to be ill as well. There was a sour taste in my mouth and I felt the first rumblings of discomfort in my stomach.

I slid down on to my side and doubled up as a pain stabbed under my heart. This was the summer fever, there could be no doubt about it. I tried to keep still, resting between bouts of pain, while the hammers thudded inside my head and my mind raced furiously. I wondered now what would happen when the Myceneans attacked, and how I was to get through the miles of enemy country even if the ambush was successful. Then there was no time to think about even this; I struggled to my knees and crawled a few paces away from the others.

Before the sickness was finished, Damon was crouching over me, holding my head. When I thought I had lost not only the food of the last hours but also of all the time since we had left Dimini, I lay back against his arm, too weak for the moment to move. Another head and shoulders blotted out the stars, and Diomedes bathed my face with a wet cloth. Then they carried me between them back to the place where we had been waiting.

I lay still with my head in my brother's lap, while my body grew quieter; then Diomedes touched my arm uncertainly, he had never seen me ill before.

"How is it now?" he asked.

"A bit easier. But Diomedes, I don't think I could stand yet, and it's nearly morning." I could feel the dawn wind cool in my damp hair, and it was lighter above the mountains. I could almost see his face.

"The king won't need a charioteer in this attack," Damon said. "When you've rested a little longer we'll get you down nearer the road, so we can collect you after the battle!"

"Oh, Damon," I said, and hid my face in his tunic, for I was ready to weep with weakness and pain, and the shame of lying hidden while Diomedes went into battle without me.

"Fool!" he said. "And you were the one who tried to teach me to see things the way they are. In an hour or two you'll be strong enough to ride again, but now if you walk you'll faint, I know these fevers. Look, we must get you to where you can rest more comfortably, and perhaps you can sleep a little."

I was sick again on the way down to the road, and shivering so that they put Damon's cloak round me as well. I dozed then, while the light grew stronger and the dry grass I lay in turned slowly green and golden.

I had not expected to sleep soundly, so I woke with a start to full daylight as feet running down the path beside me sent a patter of little stones into my face. There was the sound of men on the track below and a confused murmur of shouting and frightened horses further up the valley. I sat up, but they were out of sight behind the wall of rock to my right. The pain was almost gone now, yet the sky turned black as I stood up, and if the stone had not been close behind me I should have fallen.

There was no longer anyone below on the road, the attack must be on and I could not even see what was happening, but surely the shouting was nearer? A spear lay on the path, dropped in the rush; I reached the track leaning on it and began to totter towards the sound of fighting. I don't remember that I thought I could be of any help to Diomedes, but the idea was fixed in my head that when he was in battle I should see him fight.

A horse trailing broken reins galloped past me and I nearly fell. I had almost reached the bend when two running men broke through the tall reeds beside the track. We've won, I thought; it would be stupid to be killed by Mycenean stragglers, and I slid down behind a boulder. Then I realized that they were our own men, and from their faces I could tell that it was Thyestes' men who had won.

It was no good going on and yet I did not have the strength to go back. I crouched between two flaking grey outcrops as a wounded man in a Mycenean chariot galloped past, the horse out of control. If only I knew what had happened and if they were taking any prisoners.

The ground trembled with hoofbeats again; another chariot was coming, or more than one. This time it must really be the enemy, but I had no strength to hide. The horses slowed for the bend in the path—the driver still had them under control. I heard the wheels skid round in the dust and pulled myself to my feet, not caring who was coming so long as I knew the worst.

It was Diomedes, alone and helmetless, his hair flying back and streaked with blood. The horses were nearly on top of me and he threw all his weight back against the reins. They reared and screamed, slithering on the loose gravel, so that he could hardly hold them with both hands.

"Hipponax, get in. They're close behind," he shouted.

I got one hand on the rim of the chariot and then the dancing horses pulled it away and I fell on my knees in the road.

"Oh God, come on!" He leant far out, the whip and reins caught in one hand, reaching the other down to me. I stretched up and he caught hold of my arm, trying to lift me as I swayed to my feet, the sky turning and yellow stars in front of my eyes.

Then the horse plunged again, he lost his balance on the shifting slats of the chariot floor and fell on top of me. I heard the clatter of hooves as we rolled together over the edge of the road and down into the reed bed.

Diomedes leapt back up the bank and a few steps into the road; then he stopped and came back. "They've gone," he said flatly, his face blank with unbelief.

I tried to climb up towards him but he whipped round and looked back up the road, listening. There were more horses coming from the scene of the ambush.

"Down!"

He slithered off the track, further in among the swaying grasses. Hidden in the mat of vetch and daisies I heard the rumbling of bronze-shod wheels grow louder. The path stretched perhaps a spear's throw to the bend; one moment it lay hot and bare, the dust settling, then four chariots rounded the outcrop of rock. I watched them for perhaps two heart-beats, fully manned, regularly spaced as if they were training on a parade ground, terrible in their power. No men of Argos would escape southward now to tell those who waited below on the road to Troizen what had happened.

I dropped my head on my arms and lay motionless, feeling as bare as a mouse that has fallen into an empty wine jar, but there was no change in the rhythm of the hoofbeats. The

ground shook as they passed, the plumed leaves of the rushes blew back from the road, a powder of dust flew up from the wheels, and they were out of sight.

Diomedes tugged at me from below. "Come further in, they'll be beating the ground both sides of the track."

The stems of the great grasses, their flowerheads swaying above more than twice the height of a man, grew close together; we crawled between them till they began to thin ahead of us, and then lay flat on the grey carpet of last year's growth. I closed my eyes and dropped my head forward on my arms.

9

SCARLET POPPIES

It was quite still now except for the noise of the wind in the reeds overhead and a twittering of small brown birds. There were no more horses, no sounds of men. The aching in my head grew less as the thudding beat of my heart slowed; my mouth was dry and sour-tasting but the sickness had gone with only weakness and a little fever left. I heard Diomedes stir, and then his hand brushed the hair that straggled over my forehead. I turned on my side so that I could see his face, too weary yet to do more.

The blood in his hair seemed to come from a cut high up on his forehead; his cheeks were smeared with dirt and sweat, and it was hard to tell from his mouth that in age he was still a boy.

"Tell me," I whispered.

"I don't know what happened. The Myceneans must have known where Leander's men were all the time. A few came down the road, but they attacked mainly from the hillside above the ambush. By the time we got there our men were scattered all across the valley. They're hunting them now. It's—it's . . . like killing the rabbits in the last acre of barley."

"And Leander?"

"I don't know. I never saw him at all. He's probably dead, they can't have taken many prisoners."

There was a burst of shouting some way away, then silence again.

"How did you escape?" I asked.

"One of their chariots came straight down the track at us. I didn't know it was like that to be charged by horses when you're on foot yourself. I threw my spear and I think I must have killed the captain because when it was nearly on us it stopped suddenly. By then our men were running back past me. Damon was there, he tried to stop them with the flat of his sword. I don't remember getting into the chariot, I think it was only because I wanted to be able to see what was happening, it all seemed not real. Then they bolted and I couldn't hold them, I tried to . . . but there was the shouting. . . ."

He dropped his face into his dirty hands and pushed the fingers deep into his hair, utterly weary.

"Damon?"

"I've told you, I didn't see what happened to anyone. You don't understand, Hipponax, you weren't there." Then, more slowly, "I suppose this is the end. If Agamemnon comes it'll be too late. Thyestes' men will flow down from Mycenae like a tide and wash through to the sea; then it will be all one kingdom with only two smoking mounds to show where Argos and Tiryns were. I shall be dead then, and I'm glad I wasn't a king for any longer; it's bitter, and it hurts worse than any pain I've ever dreamed of."

I pushed myself up on to one elbow. "And who are you, Diomedes," I said, "to tell the Gods that you are no longer a king? Men are dead in this valley, but we are still alive in it, and Leander may be safe in the mountains. Even if he isn't, who from Mycenae yet knows that you aren't in your own palace, and while Thyestes thinks you're there he won't attack. It's eight days yet till the moon changes. Before there were lots of different things that you had to do because you were a king, now there's only one. You must stay alive by any way you can, and for as long as you can till the news comes from Sparta or the Gods show us some way you can get back to your people."

"You thought this was foolishness all along, didn't you Hipponax; why?"

I told him then what Damon had told me on the night of the council, and of Chryseis' warning. He looked at me strangely.

"Why didn't you tell me this then?"

"Would you have listened?"

"Yes. No, I suppose not willingly, but you could have made me."

"Could I, Diomedes? You were the king, remember, very much the king." Then, as he turned away quickly so that I should not see his face, "Hush, I was wrong, we both were, and now this morning and only this morning I can be sure why. There isn't any other way we could have been betrayed."

"I still don't understand. I can't think properly."

"Who was the one person who knew exactly what happened at our councils and yet was in no danger herself? The Lady Persea! You have never thought, Diomedes, how little reason she has to love you; for all the years since Adrastus' wife died she has been almost a queen in Argos. She is not a stupid women, nor a simple one, she knows that she could rule a kingdom such as this. Set aside as she has been, she has no reason to show reverence to men, whether they are kings, or the princes who always seem to spring up to succeed them."

"You mean that because she felt like that she betrayed us to Thyestes? But he would have wanted Argos for himself."

"Even if he ruled the whole land Mycenae would still be the citadel of the High King. Alone in Argos Persea would have had all the power she needed."

"And now she's won. I still don't understand how, or really why, but I expect it won't be long now before Thyestes' men find us."

We rested for a while, as the sun rose higher and beat down through the thin stems of the reeds. I looked at the small grey snails clustered on the reed stalks, and at a column of ants clearing a road through the grass, anything to keep my thoughts steady. My lips were dry and I began to think about water, fresh from the pottery cooler, or running over rocks from a stream in the mountains. I knew I must drink soon, the sickness had emptied me so that in this heat I could not go as long without water as a fit man; without it the fever would mount and Diomedes would be alone with a delirious man. I sat up slowly.

Diomedes looked across at me. "Are you going to be sick again?"

"No, but we must find something to drink."

He looked round helplessly; our water bottles were lost above on the road, and the stream bed was dry.

"There must be water somewhere," he said, "or these reeds wouldn't still be green. I think there was a patch of fresh green back up the valley; there must be a spring there."

"Could we reach it under cover of the reeds?"

"We'll have to try. Can you crawl, Hipponax? Better to go now and drink than lie here all day and be taken at the end. You were right, you know, in what you said just now. I can even see now why I didn't understand better when we were making our plans; but why must it cost us all our lives for me to learn even that much?"

"Don't talk now about what you've learned and what you haven't," I said. "If we both live to the new moon we can discuss it more fully over a bowl of wine in Argos."

"If it's so important that I've got to stay alive, it matters to me that you do too. Let me help you, Hipponax."

We could not go very fast, I was too weak, and we stopped often to listen for the sounds of a search. The sweat ran into my eyes and my arms and legs began to tremble. Before we reached the end of the reedbed I stopped, sat back on my heels, and loosened the straps of my armour.

"It's no good to me now," I said, "and I can't stand the weight. Better take yours off too."

The dry air was cool and delicious against my body as I shook out the tunic which the sweat had plastered flat to my skin. Ahead through the reeds there were greener leaves and a patch of crimson. Diomedes had been right about the spring; it rose deep in a cleft of rock, dripping down through a smear of moss to vanish into the gravel. Below it was a small open place where the spring flowers were still bright and a drift of poppies grew up from among the low green leaves. I looked carefully but there seemed to be no one hidden anywhere near and no sound but the chirp of the small birds. We half-ran, half-crawled to the shelter of the rocks ahead.

I drank slowly because the water was cold, and between times let it play on my neck and arms. When it had made me shiver I moved out into the sun again, feeling clearer-headed and stronger than I had for hours. A low brown boulder lay in the poppies to my right. I watched it lazily as the warmth soaked back and the hot sun dried my wet tunic; then it began to puzzle me. It was the wrong colour; the rocks behind us where the wild bees were drinking from the wet stone were grey streaked with orange.

I half-raised myself to see better. There was a twist of cloth, a different red from the poppies, caught around the stone. I knew then what it was that lay so still among the flowers, and my face as I turned to Diomedes showed him what I had seen.

He reached the body before I did; the tunic the colour of Argos was torn back from the bare ribs that had looked like stone. The head was twisted to one side with long red hair blown across the face. Diomedes smoothed it back and I knew my brother Damon.

We knelt one on either side of him. The marks on his body

showed clearly what had happened—the cut on his right shoulder that he had loosened his tunic to bathe, and the deep spearthrust through the neck that had killed him as he knelt at the spring. It was the body of my brave, quiet, younger brother, but I felt nothing as we straightened his limbs and washed the blood from his face. It seemed to me that his life was still very near us and the body it had worn, or perhaps it was only that I knew my own death might be so close that only a few moments more separated us. If a time ever came when I could tell my father what I had seen, I knew I should grieve then.

A fly settled on Damon's face and I brushed it away. There must be many bodies in the valley; soon the vultures would be here, and the small beasts that live on carrion.

"Can we bury him?" Diomedes asked.

"Not deep, but we must cover him from the flies," I said.

We lifted the body out from the poppies and laid it in a hollow of clean sand. I covered it with torn handfuls of hemlock and yellow ragwort before we piled small stones from the stream bed over the legs. Before Damon was quite covered Diomedes stopped.

"Leander's dagger. I don't want Thyestes' men to have it. If there's ever a time when we can bury him properly I can take it again."

He drew the long knife from its sheath and held it so that the light flashed on the tiny lions, before clearing a place among the dying flowers so that it lay by my brother's hands.

When there was nothing more that we could do we drank again and rested. Diomedes took my cold fingers and squeezed them, looking at me in the hurt way boys have when they must watch someone they know in pain, before they learn there are some hurts no one can cure. Yet my mind was still numb and I felt very little, no final end to a good thing in my life that had been mine for as long as I could remember.

I said, "We must get away from here, they're bound to search the spring again, and we might be able to get down the valley now to the Troizen road." Then I saw that it was already too late.

A soldier pushed his way through the reeds ahead of us, and as we jumped up there were nodding crests to left and right as well. The first man shouted and they closed in. Diomedes' hand went to the empty scabbard of his dagger, but I knocked it down, standing against the wet rock, my hands open in front of me. There was no way to escape and I must keep Diomedes living by any way I could think of for as long as maybe.

It was hard to stand still while rough hands searched for concealed weapons before we were prodded out into the open with spear butts and driven towards the road. A chariot stood there, twisted sideways as the restless horses reached for the weeds on the far side. A Mycenean captain sat at his ease on the floor of the chariot, drinking from a leather bottle, while his men leaned on their spears, laughing with the easy complacency of soldiers who have done better than they expected to; none of them seemed to be wounded.

A thick rope was knotted to the axle of the chariot; it trailed some way in the dust among the huddle of prisoners who crouched there, bound to it in pairs. There were not more than ten or twelve.

The captain jerked his head towards the rope without speaking when he saw us, but a man shouted, "I thought we cleared the stream bed long ago."

"These are the last."

I fell to my knees as the guard kicked from behind. He kicked again and I stumbled towards the rope. Close behind the chariot a young man in saffron rags lay in the dust while the prisoner behind him tried with bound hands to stem the blood that oozed from a leg wound. Neither saw us as we passed, but I gripped Diomedes' arm for support and to keep him silent. After the guard had finished with us I edged sideways so that I could see again; Diomedes was staring at me, his eyes enormous with the question he dared not ask. I nodded "yes".

So Leander was alive but hurt. How long would a wounded man keep up as we were driven back to Mycenae? I had not expected him to be living after the disastrous ambush, for only those on the edge of the fighting would have had much chance of getting clear, and Leander of Tiryns would not have been among them. Perhaps his wound explained what had happened. I had hoped he lay quiet with Damon under the wide sky, not that I must see him die like an illtreated beast while I watch with bound hands.

The captain got up, wiped his mouth with the back of his hand, and did up the loosened strap of his helmet.

"Get the men back here," he said to his squire. "It's uphill most of the way home."

The youth blew three blasts on the cow-horn slung at his belt, and counted the last stragglers as they came back out of the undergrowth. "All here," he said.

A guard jerked on the rope that held us, and we struggled to our feet. I could not see Leander now past the backs ahead of us. We were the last in the line, nearest the guards, and I hoped the citadel of Mycenae was not as far away as I remembered.

The horses were tired and the chariot clattered slowly over the uneven ground, otherwise I should have had no chance. While we were moving I knew that Leander must still be on his feet, and I think that was what kept me on mine. The guards were laughing still, but we marched with bent heads, watching the feet next ahead of us in the dust, watching for a sudden pull on the rope that could have us down, watching the lazy curl of the horse-whip that snaked about our dirty legs. I did not raise my eyes once to the pass at the head of the valley; behind it would be another, behind that I did not know. Better to think only of the next few steps, as far as the twisted bush, now twenty paces to the rock on the left, now as far as the giant thistles growing across the path. We passed the place of the ambush, with the last of the bodies and a broken chariot, then the track grew even worse as it twisted upwards. We stopped once on the hillside, one of the prisoners was down, but I could not see who. Then we went on again.

I was still counting my steps a long time later, hunched up and staggering like an old man, when Diomedes pushed me with his elbow. I raised my aching head and tried to follow where he was looking through the choking dust. Two cone-shaped mountains rose one on either side of us, and as the road dropped away between them I saw in the cleft the citadel of Mycenae on its tongue of rock, sprawling and unfamiliar seen from behind. It was late afternoon with the sun in our eyes, and the tiered roofs ahead were edged with gold. The guards cheered, and I began to hope that after all we should reach it alive.

100

It was still a long while before we were clear of the mountains, and then the path led round north of the citadel, divided from it by a steep ravine, for there was only a small postern gate to the rear of the fortress; the main entrance faced west.

We reached the paved way that ran round under the curve of the walls as the road did at Argos. They sloped up to the left, unbroken, enormous, the great foundation stones the height of a man, fitting closely to each other like the edges of a broken pot. Then a shadow darkened the road and we were between walls on both sides, for ahead rose the great gate. The stone lionesses that reared above it snarled straight into the lowering sun, pawing the column that stood between them, the Standing Lions of Mycenae, tokens of the High King. The captain in his chariot raised his spear in greeting as he clattered over the wheel grooves in the stone threshold and into the dark tunnel that led up under the wall; and I thought of Diomedes' dagger, hidden now, but perhaps not for ever.

10

BENEATH THE LIONS

No light came now from the shaft that sloped upwards through the thickness of the stone. There was a torch beyond the wooden grating that closed the far end of the vault built into the foundations of the citadel, but it showed no more than the shapes of the men who lay around me. I had propped myself against the roots of the wall, twisted round into the position that seemed at the moment to be easing the cramping pains in my stomach; Leander lay with his head in Diomedes' lap. A great water jar stood between the squat pillars which supported the roof, and from time to time one of the men crawled over to it, awkward with his chained legs, and drank from the dipper. It was nearly empty now and it did not seem likely that there would be any more before morning. The guard outside changed; the captain glanced at us through the grating and turned away.

Diomedes stretched, trying not to disturb the weight that lay across his knees.

"Can't you sleep?" I asked. "Nothing will happen tonight."

"I haven't tried yet."

Leander said, "Then try now, and I hope I can sleep with you."

His voice was still uncertain, jerky with pain. He had been unconscious for more than an hour after we had at last been herded into our prison. I felt across towards his injured leg;

the rags we had tied over the place where a horse had kicked him were slipping again, and the wound felt hot and swollen. I wetted the dressing with almost the last of the water and retied it.

Leander said through gritted teeth, "I've got two legs, why must the horse kick that one?"

"If he hadn't you wouldn't have got to Mycenae; one good and one bad are better than two which won't hold you up," said Diomedes.

Then Ion, one of our men, not much older than Diomedes, asked the question that was in all our minds. "Lord King, what will happen in the morning?"

Quickly Diomedes eased Leander's head off his knees and turned so that he could reach Ion, pulling him over by the shoulders. "Call me any name you like, anything except 'Diomedes' or 'Lord King'. Don't you understand? It's not just to save my life, but if Thyestes discovers that he has two kings in his prison what will happen to Argos?" He shook the boy and let him go.

Ion stammered, "I didn't think. It's hard, you see, I've never been so close to you before, and now . . . even that's enough to make me forget how I ought to speak."

"That's one feeling which won't last," said Diomedes, and I could tell by his voice that he was smiling. "How many are we? Thirteen? When thirteen men are shut up as close together as we are here some differences don't matter for very long. We're all hungry and sore and frightened."

"But what do you think will happen in the morning?" persisted another voice.

"I don't know, but there wasn't much point keeping us alive this long only to kill us tomorrow. He may want information, but how can we give him that? Aren't we all common soldiers? How do we know why we were marched to the east valley, we can't see into the minds of kings! The best thing we can do

104

tonight is to sleep while we can and let the future look after itself. We've had the luck to stay alive; that may not be the end of it. Sleep well."

He turned away from the listening men and lay down beside Leander. The three of us were now a little apart from the others, huddled on the stone floor covered with gritty sand; what straw there had been we had swept away into a corner, it was too foul to lie on. I lay on my back for a while, and when that began to ache shifted almost over with my head resting on my arms. Leander could not move as easily and I heard him gasp and catch his breath as he turned on to one side. Then he and Diomedes began whispering together.

"You said that well."

"Did I? I wish I'd believed it myself."

"That doesn't matter as long as the men did."

"Thyestes won't let it go so easily, will he? There'll be things he wants to know."

"I suppose so."

"What can we do, Leander? No, that's a silly thing to ask. We shall have to do the best we can. I'm glad Hipponax made me throw my armour away, at least we don't look like kings. That may give us a little time."

"Now hush, it won't be long till dawn. Turn round, then I can lie against your back."

I suppose I had slept for about two hours when the fever woke me again. I was burning and the tunic was sticking to my back till I moved, then the chill from the stone floor struck upwards and I began to shiver so much that my teeth rattled and I thought everyone in the prison would wake. I tried to pull my mind free from the enormous distorted thoughts of fever and found I was still in a waking nightmare. Thyestes would go for the weakest links when he began his questioning, those of us who were hurt already. The men I could not speak for but Leander knew pain with an old companionship; his mind was skilled in the desperate arts that a man may learn when his body has become an alien thing to be used in a battle against his spirit. It was of myself that I was not sure.

I had not known that he was awake until he said very softly, "Are you cold, Hipponax? Come closer to me."

"It's only the fever. Have you slept, Leander?"

"Not what I'd call sleep in the ordinary way, but I wouldn't have expected that."

He was lying with his back partly towards me, speaking over his shoulder. I moved so that he lay against my breast, I could take some of the weight of his body and we were warmer like that. His skin smelt of sweat and dust, and the dried blood on his bandages. The whole cell was foul, and I half-remembered that through my nightmares some of the men had been restless. They were all quiet now. High up from the slit in the wall came the hoot of an owl, and then the thin cry of the first cock.

Diomedes turned and threw out an arm in his sleep.

"Things couldn't be much worse, could they?" Leander said quietly. "I've been thinking. Even if Achates brings Agamemnon back to Argos they won't know about us, and little kingdoms like ours depend on their kings. I suppose Achates and Mecistheos will lead our men, but it won't be the same. Diomedes asked once before if this was the end of the old pattern; I think now that it must be, because even if Agamemnon wins, Tiryns and Argos won't ever be what they were before. It's funny, Hipponax, I don't think in those two years when I was king that I was ever happy in the way Diomedes must have been with you at Dimini, but now if I could have just one of those days back again, one without pain. . . ."

"Leander, your leg will heal, the pain will go." It was Diomedes.

"You should be asleep, did we wake you?" I whispered.

106

"I don't know. I wasn't asleep really, and I heard my name. Leander sounded so final."

"It helps sometimes to see things really clearly. Diomedes, I know that unless the Mistress stretches out her own hand and plucks me out herself I shan't come out of here alive. . . ."

"Leander!"

"No, hush. Wounds like mine heal, but not among this filth. Oh, I can ride my chariot and fight and seem strong enough, but the body doesn't forget treatment like mine had two years ago. Look, I'm not saying this out of pity for myself, but because now you're awake there's something we've got to talk about while we can. Shift me up against the wall, Hipponax. I can't think like this."

Between us we got him arranged more comfortably against my shoulder. "Listen," he said then, in his strange voice which was harsh and breathless at the same time. "I seem to be seeing things clearly tonight, perhaps I'm getting fever like Hipponax. It may be this is really the end, the end for us, and that's all we shall care about then. Yet even now, even when we're helpless, something may happen. Diomedes, you might escape. . . ."

"But how?"

"Let me finish. I don't know how; perhaps Thyestes is mad, perhaps he'll let you go of his own accord or give you a chance to escape. If, if that should happen, you must be both of us then, in both the kingdoms. We're both wiser now than we were and I think we're seeing things more clearly. Surely that must help if only one of us could get back. Even Hipponax."

Knowing in my own heart that it could not be me either I said, "Yes, I think I see."

"It's important for us to understand this now," he went on, "because we may not get another chance to talk like this, with the others asleep," and I saw behind his words that this was not the full reason. He was trying with what strength he had left to lead Diomedes as a man gentles a frightened horse over a narrow bridge. Only by going beyond the worst and seeing what was there could he live through the next days. And Diomedes must live.

"They don't know about the Lady Persea," I said.

"Your cousin does," whispered Diomedes.

"Who would believe Chryseis, even if she could find a way to speak to anyone important?"

"I wasn't only thinking of what you told me about Persea earlier tonight," said Leander. "But that was part of it. Do you see, Diomedes? It might feel harder, if one of us got the chance, to go and leave the others than to stay, but that mustn't be allowed to happen."

"Yes."

I saw that Diomedes had taken Leander's hand. For a little while we all lay quietly. There did not seem to be anything left to be said, and as Leander's words penetrated deeper into my mind they brought with them a curious lightness. It did indeed help, when your body was chained to a wall, to set the mind free to walk forwards and then back down all the paths that might lie ahead.

Then Diomedes gave a little chuckle. It was such an unlikely sound to hear that for one moment I thought he was crying.

"Tell us," whispered Leander.

"It wasn't funny really, only rather strange. I was thinking that I suppose this is the worst thing that ever happened to me, and then I remembered the times I'd thought that before about other things. Hipponax, do you remember Philon— the time we first saw him?"

"Yes of course."

"Did it remind you of when my father died?"

"I thought you remembered it then."

"It was like this, Leander. You asked me once how I remembered my father, and I told you with love and a little awe. I was ten when he died, and I think no other death after that one will ever be quite so bad. I suppose when it happens, the first of anything is the worst time because there's nothing to compare it with. I remember waving when he rode away to fight at Thebes, but I never thought I wouldn't see him again; I was much too concerned with how he looked in his blue cloak, and the things he'd tried to say before he went. I'd known they were very important but it's hard to listen when you're ten and very excited, and now I can't even remember his voice."

"Yours is getting very like it," I said.

"Is it? I rather thought it must be, because of the way I seem able to shout now. I know his voice carried well. Leander, when the messenger came back from Thebes it was like the house falling on me. I remember he came late in the afternoon and I was in the kitchen yard playing with the new puppy. There was the wailing, and then the cook ran out towards me and stopped half-way with her hands over her mouth and scuttled back into the house. That really frightened me; it was as if I was suddenly put apart from everyone else, which was more alarming than anything. Of course she was right in a way, because a great sorrow does set people apart. I suppose she'd been going to tell me, and then realized that it wasn't for her to do it."

"Who did?" asked Leander.

"Hipponax' father, old Bias, but I wouldn't listen. He was trying to explain and I ran out of the hall. It was because he couldn't keep his voice steady, and I'd never known that a man of his size could cry."

I remembered that evening with a sudden painful clearness: the ugly sound of weeping coming from the women's rooms, my father's face as he stood looking at the empty master's chair in the hall, the bewildered young messenger, drooping exhausted and forgotten. It was after I had taken him to the kitchen to be fed that I had found Diomedes.

"You hid behind a pillar in the courtyard," I said. "I thought you were the new puppy when I heard you snuffling. I was only just back from my spell of guard duty at Argos and I'd rather forgotten about you."

"I think I felt like a whipped puppy." Diomedes was smiling again. "You came and made a comforting noise, and then when you saw who it was you picked me up, and then things weren't so bad."

"And so that wasn't the day on which the world came to an end after all, and tomorrow may not be the day either," said Leander. "No, I suppose it's today now, it's nearly morning. At least we aren't alone, though I think loneliness isn't being where there are no people. If friends are separated they can still have the strength of being one of two; and do you re-member, I don't think I've ever felt quite so apart as when I've been drawn up on a battlefield among a thousand strangers."

I touched Leander's bare shoulder. Suddenly, in the moment of peace after he had finished speaking, Diomedes had fallen asleep.

11

THE HALL OF THYESTES

THE morning sunlight was like a blow in the face as we were driven up into the main courtyard of the citadel. There was no time, as I rubbed my eyes with bound hands, except to see that because the rock beneath rose very steeply it seemed smaller and more irregularly shaped than ours at Argos; then the porch of the great hall was ahead. I was sure that it was magnificent, but slaves and prisoners do not raise their eyes to noble carving, they count the steps so that if their trembling will let them, they may mount without falling. Within the welcome shadow I saw only the seething multitude of captains, lords and courtiers who clustered around the pillars, shifting and humming like bees about a hive on a spring day, shining and metalled as bees, with fine worked armour and swords to sting.

The king's seat was to the right, according to custom, so that he might not be too quickly seen. The voices hushed as the guard halted us in the clear space below him. We were a small dishevelled group, Leander not able to stand alone, Diomedes an awkward sullen farm boy to any who noticed him, the men frightened—for the guards had not brought us up gently from the prison. A spear butt prodded me in the ribs and I fell on my knees; the fever was high again.

"A pitiful collection!" said a voice, cold and beyond the reach of pity. I looked up for the first time into the face of the High King.

I knew then why he had not led his own men against us in the fighting for Gelanor's manor. He sat, twisted sideways on his plaster seat in front of the painted griffons, wrapped in a great robe of dark red; and this was a dying man. He was not yet old and his hair was dark, yet it hung round his face in thin curls, sparse and clinging to the skull. The face itself was like a puppet's, shrunken and yellow with the lips in a bitter line. It was a mouth that could once have been generous as the hands had been strong; now the High King was gripped by a power greater than his own. I wondered what his life had been that he should want to spend its last months in battle and bloodshed, rather than resting quietly in the contemplation of his royal years.

The yellow eyes passed over us one by one, as we knelt before him. I bowed my head over the octopus painted on the square of floor in front of me. It had a face with a cruel beak that was a mirror of Thyestes.

"That man in front, no, the redhead. Bring him here."

It was Ion; two of the guards dragged him up the three steps to the platform in front of the king's seat.

"You are from Argos?"

The boy nodded, helpless and trembling.

"How did you come to be in the east valley yesterday?"

"I don't know." The guard kicked him. "How could I know? I went under orders, I couldn't help myself."

"Whose orders?"

"My captain's. Damon of the guard."

"And who commanded you?"

"Damon."

"Fool." Thyestes struck out with the cane that was clutched between his fingers. "I know that Damon commands only fifty. Would you have me believe that he led more than twice that number yesterday across my land?"

"The others were from Tiryns, how should I know who

112

they were? It was dark when we were ordered out, I didn't even see their faces."

"You may be a fool who is telling the truth, or a liar. We will discover later; take him back."

Ion stumbled down the steps and fell, helpless with bound hands. I hoped he realized that he had done well. Now Thyestes was looking from face to face again; the stick stabbed towards Leander.

"Him."

A guard jerked at him, but Leander could not stand. His right leg gave way and he hung from the man's hands, a trickle of fresh blood running from below the bandages. The guard had dragged him two steps forward before it came loose altogether and slid down his leg to the floor.

I had not seen the Cretan standing a little to one side of the king's seat in the shadows. I knew him now again as he came down the steps and out into the light that streamed from the upper galleries; it gleamed on the polished skin of his body and the chains about his neck as he stood looking down at Leander. The young king's ribs heaved beneath the yellow shreds of his tunic and his face was hidden in a tangle of dark hair. The Cretan lifted the rags aside with the toe of one gilded boot.

The double scar of the old wound still showed on Leander's leg through the blood and bruising of the new.

"Do you see, my Lord King? Can there be two scars like that in Tiryns?" He dropped the tunic fastidiously and looked towards Thyestes, one eyebrow raised.

"Show me his face."

The captain of the guard took Leander by the shoulders and pulled him up, half-kneeling on the floor. The Cretan brushed the hair back.

"Leander of Tiryns, this is a strange embassy on which you come to your overlord. You would have had a kinder welcome if you had ridden in peace up to the Lion Gate, and not crept across my border like a mouse into a grain store."

"How else should I come against a High King who invades my land without cause?" said Leander through his teeth.

"Your land? Well, perhaps we may have let you think so. It seems that for too long I have been like a man sleeping in the house who hears the playing of children through his dreams. Now they have grown rough and woken him, and he must stir himself to drive them away."

Leander was silent, and the Cretan let his head fall forward again. Then he laughed, a mirthless sound, suddenly loud in the waiting silence of the hall.

"Look at this king, my lords and captains! He is no more than a dirty, frightened boy with a bloody nose, who must be sent home where he belongs. Lord King, you have no need of crippled serfs, send him back to his people. It is a small gift."

This was something quite new, one more tangle in the ravelled skein of Thyestes' plan. What could be in the Cretan's mind? Surely even the High King could see that there was danger in this? Perhaps the Cretan was after all not so secure in his success as he seemed, and even now in what had seemed our darkest misery there was a crack of light; as if the Cretan was thinking to himself that one day it might matter, it might be a way of escape, that he had let Leander go. I wondered if Thyestes would see this, but when he spoke I knew that he had not.

"Why not? There will be enough slaves in Mycenae and to trade across the sea before the moon is full again. I will send this princeling home to be nursed or left to die as his people will—and any others who are wounded, unless it should chance that there are other kings among them?"

I froze motionless, not daring to raise my eyes to where Diomedes was kneeling in front of me; I could feel the thoughts of the other prisoners. Could not the High King tell? Could he not see in our faces? The hope that had sprung up with the thought of Leander free in Argos wavered like a flame that dies in a sudden draught.

There was a hum of sound around the hall and some laughter. The High King was in a good humour today and the sight of Leander of Tiryns bleeding on the floor had been an unlooked-for diversion. It was too much to hope that such a miserable group of prisoners should hold any further surprises.

The king had turned aside to talk to one of the captains while the Cretan walked among the prisoners. One of the Tirynians had a broken arm, he motioned for him to be put on one side with Leander. Then the elegant boots stopped before me.

"This one's shaking. Is he ill?"

The captain held me up limply like a half-empty sack of corn.

"Yes, he's hot with fever. There'll be no profit to be made from him after a few more days in the prisons of Mycenae."

"Throw him back into the sea with the other little fish, then. I suppose I must find a cart to send them back in. Lock the rest up securely though, the king's generosity mustn't be abused." The Cretan turned on his heel, laughing, and stepped lightly back on to the dais by the king's throne.

Thyestes turned towards him, about to speak. Then his face changed, his mouth fell open in a soundless cry, and he twisted sideways over the arm of his seat. The Cretan jumped to catch him as he began to slide to the ground, the king's hands clung to his arms and they swayed together in the frightened silence. Then the spasm that had seized Thyestes seemed to pass and his squire laid him back, his skin leaden against the purple coverings thrown across the chair.

The guards who had been about to take us from the hall
115

stood uncertain. Now the Cretan gestured to them impatiently, and to the other courtiers.

"The king must rest."

"Wait." The yellow hand reached for the jewelled cane

116

which had slid to the ground. The Cretan stooped and picked it up.

"Show me the prisoners again. No, closer, it's dark, I can't see. The priestess said. . . ."

The ten men with Diomedes among them were brought back to the foot of the steps. The king peered at them, still weak, supported by the Cretan.

"She said that we must wait till the new moon," he muttered. "But what will have changed by then? We had them ready to break, but she said wait. Ten more days and they will break themselves. You hear that, Leander? Your friend was not found, unless the vultures reached him before we did. There's no Diomedes to scuttle back to and plot with again. He's dead, or run away like the country boy he is."

His eyes flickered along the row of prisoners, past Diomedes standing sullenly, then back again.

"A country boy, that boy there, the one with the fair hair. Bring him nearer."

Diomedes' shoulders had straightened and the lines of his face changed and grown firmer even before the guard reached him.

"I had thought you were so little a king, Thyestes, that you could not recognize the royal blood when you saw it," he said.

The lips twisted in the pain-marred face above him and I realized that Thyestes was trying to smile. "So she was right, the priestess. I waited and the Mistress brought me what I asked for. Has life been so evil for you, Diomedes of Argos, that you must draw your death towards you with both hands?"

Diomedes did not answer, but the Cretan bent forward and spoke in the king's ear. "Lord Thyestes, you have them both now, the two kingdoms are yours. Give the word and our men will burn Argos at nightfall and Tiryns in the dawn."

"No, there are still the days to the new moon. How many? I can't remember, but it's at the waxing of the moon that the kingdoms will change, that's what the priestess said. 'The riderless chariot, he who is wise like the Gods will seize it and the kingdoms will be made again under its wheels.' I am Thyestes, my name is the grinder that crushes the corn. Let Leander go, what can he do alone? If he should fight for Argos himself in the days that are left, so much the better. We shall take the riderless chariot from hands that are already weakened when the day comes. No, you, Diomedes, shall lie in chains below my palace and learn in truth that you are a king no longer, while the ally you thought you could trust gathers strength to take over your kingdom. Who knows, he may sleep for one night in your bed before I burn Argos over his body."

I could not struggle or cry out in any voice that would reach him as Diomedes, quiet, his eyes seeing nothing around him, was taken out of the hall with the other prisoners.

"Live while you can, king of Argos," the Cretan shouted after him. "It is cold to lie on stone, but colder beneath it; and the corn grows, they say, from the blood of kings!"

The guards came back for those of us who were to be let free. We waited a long, thirsty time, out in the hot sun of the lower courtyard. I sat back to back with the wounded Tirynian, while Leander leaned against my knees, and now that my hands were free I could bind up his leg again. I think it is the stupidity of shackled hands that first cuts into the numb mind of a prisoner with a warning of what lies ahead. Now my hands had been loosed. We did not talk to each other because there was nothing yet that we could say, with those walls around us.

Leander's mind seemed very far away, though whether because of the pain in his body or for my own reason I did not know him well enough to be sure. His face was shut and grave

118

as it had been the first day we had met him on the battlefield below Mecistheos' orchards. During his short friendship with Diomedes he had changed and blossomed; now he was alone again, and before night fell he would lie between linen sheets while his friend endured the stench and darkness of the High King's prison, and perhaps more.

I sat and gazed up at the strength of the walls, at the palace rising higher than I could see, painted white and blue and red, the great roofbeams and the windowframes carved and gilded. I thought of the wealth of gold and jewels worn by the palace women, the arms of the men, the bronze and oil and corn below in the storerooms. The least of the courtiers here drank from goblets as magnificent as the one Diomedes used at Argos, and the bowl in which the wine was mixed, flowering with lilies and girdled with fishes of azure and green, was more beautiful than any I had seen before. But the men of Mycenae could not understand what Diomedes had known ever since he was a child—that loyalty is stronger than gold, stronger even than reason, and may lead men into deeds that are more enduring than stone.

Leander's words of the night before had been turned back on himself. He could never have guessed that he might be the one to be free; now he must hold to his side of the bargain and I knew that I must help him as Diomedes would have wished me to. Though the two kings were divided by the walls of Mycenae their men would still fight as one when the day of the full moon came. I could not bear to think yet of the hours I must live through till then.

A cart, its wheels still clogged with the last of the season's hay, clattered across the worn paving stones, and I shuffled to my feet. Leander lay on the ground until he was lifted in after us. The marching feet of the escort echoed under the arch and there was a derisive cheer from the walls as we rolled out into the sunlight.

119

I settled myself against the high side of the cart so that I would not have to look back at the walls of Mycenae rising behind us as we drove down among the houses. Leander's voice, irregular with the jolting of the cart, surprised me.

"He won't live long, Hipponax."

"Who?" My mind was still full of Diomedes, it was not a habit to be thrown off quickly.

"Thyestes, of course, and she'll know that—the priestess. Now why? Did he use her or she him? Don't you see, I think whatever it was that they planned, it's going wrong. Something bad always breaks in the end because it's the wrong shape."

"Damon said that."

"Did he? Yes, I suppose he knew first because he's been in the palace longer. Persea thinks Thyestes will do as she says and then die, and who knows what horrors she has planned ready for that day, for she wants far more than Argos. And, Hipponax, it won't work. I can feel that it won't. The priestess isn't the power she uses, it'll leave her even as it's leaving Thyestes, so that he's mad enough to let us go."

I knew he was right, but now a little of my mind was pulling free, going ahead of the slow cart to Argos and Chryseis who had watched there these last two nights, and to the cleansing that lay ahead of us.

A group of peasants stood open-mouthed to stare as we came out into the open country again. I stared back at them, then, looking away, gripped Leander's shoulder so that he grunted in hurt surprise, for one of them—a grubby and quite unnoteworthy little boy—had been Philon.

12

WIND FROM THE SOUTH

IT was evening, and I was leaning wearily against a pillar of the great portico near the entrance of the women's rooms. The air felt stale and heavy, with little gusts of wind coming from no one way more than another and picking up the dust. Mecistheos waited in the shadows behind me with a detail of men; the business we were about was one that must be done before we could sleep again with any sort of safety, yet only my hunger to see Chryseis safe and unharmed was keeping me on my feet.

There was a stir beyond the archway, the sound of a pattern of clear pipe notes and the rhythm of a little drum. A group of palace ladies, dressed for a sacrifice, came out into the last of the daylight. Behind them were servants with covered baskets and vases, and the Lady Persea, her gold-trimmed flounces tinkling in time to the music as she glided out looking neither to left nor right.

I could not see Chryseis and the hair rose on the back of my neck as I thought what could have already been done to her. Then she came out, almost the last among the attendants.

As the High Priestess moved into the courtyard Mecistheos stepped forward. Two of his men went quickly to close the doors of the smaller courtyard behind the women, while others halted the leaders. The drum beats faltered and stopped.

"Lady Persea, where are you going?" Mecistheos stepped directly in front of the High Priestess, whose face did not change—as if she saw only empty air before her.

One of the ladies answered. "We go to offer sacrifice to the Mistress for the men who will soon fight in her name."

"Have you leave from the king to go to the Holy Place outside the walls of the citadel at such a time of danger?"

"If the danger is so great then what better time is there for us to do our work?" asked the woman crossly, but her eyes were frightened.

"The king would not have you cut down by enemy chariot wheels, and which of us knows for sure when the High King will attack? It has been commanded that worship is to be made within the walls of the palace," said Mecistheos.

"By whom? What king is there to give orders now?"

"Leander of Tiryns, and his word will be obeyed by you as by us all, according to the wishes of King Diomedes."

The Lady Persea turned, her face still expressionless, and her women went with her, straggling back towards the closed doors.

"No, you cannot enter. The king finds that the hall of the women is no longer safe, and has arranged that other rooms be found for the Lady Persea and her attendants while they are repaired. My men will show you."

Persea spun round, the ugly colour rising up her breast and throat as she swept towards Mecistheos. Two guards jumped forward, their faces showing their unwillingness to touch a priestess, but they were not needed. Her attendants caught hold of the heavy flounces of her skirt to hold her back and the older women closed about the small, brilliant figure. As the guards began to lead the whole party away, I caught Chryseis by the arm and pulled her towards me. A guard turned, then at a look from Mecistheos left us together.

"No," I said. "Not any more. I won't have you with that witch any longer."

Chryseis started to cry. "Hipponax, what's happening? Where are they taking them?"

122

"Only where they can be securely guarded until it's too late to get another message to Thyestes. Oh yes, Chryseis, Mecistheos knows now about the secret passage under the wall from the priestess's room."

"Then it will be all right, really safe? The men won't ride out to an enemy who are waiting again? Only Diomedes . . . but you came back, Hipponax." She buried her face against my shoulder.

Mecistheos had gone through into the courtyard to bring out the last of the women; now they were gone it would be quiet there in the twilight, with golden fish swimming in the tank in the middle. Suddenly the palace seemed full of eyes; I turned Chryseis, with my arm still round her, and we went in. Chryseis looked up at the open doors of the empty rooms and I could feel her trembling.

"Has it been bad?"

"Yes, I think the lady suspected that I'd told you something. She didn't harm me but I thought all the time she was going to, and last night Philon disappeared, so that I couldn't have got a message out if I'd wanted to. Hipponax, I've seen her punish people; there was Latromis."

"Latromis?"

"Yes, she's dead. I don't know what happened to her body, but I heard the women talking. They must have known that she'd spoken about what happened at the grove before the first attack."

"So that was how it was done, messages sent from the grove by any one of the initiates. When Argos is clean again, we'll find out where Latromis is buried and she shall have a grave and tomb clothes as fine as any lady in the land." My arm tightened around her.

"So it isn't too late, Hipponax, even though Thyestes has Diomedes at Mycenae?"

"No. I don't know why I'm so sure, it may be because of

the fever, but I think things are going even worse for Thyestes than they are for us. The High King is dying, Chryseis, and it's dreadful to see even such a man ill in that way and twisted in his mind at the same time. Persea knows all this; though we'll never find out how long she plotted, and how the women passed back and forward between the holy places as the plan became more and more exact. You said once that people were trying to make us believe that the Gods were fighting against us; what Persea believes in her heart only the Mistress will ever know, but Thyestes trusts her. She has given him a prophecy of triumph, and now he will hold fast to it even though waiting till the new moon may mean he attacks too late."

"It's like the layers coming away when you peel an onion. Perhaps she had other plans for what was to happen at the new moon. Hipponax, I understand her a little better now; all the time I've been in the citadel she's been winding herself closer and tighter round one idea, waiting till she could break out and make everything different, the Argos it would have become if women ruled."

"Isn't it possible that the Mistress may still give her the power to do it? Diomedes may not come out of Mycenae alive."

"No, Hipponax." Her eyes were suddenly very bright and certain in the fading light. "I am a woman; the Mistress all women venerate is a true god, and may be even more powerful than the Horse King the warriors pour blood to. But she is a power to flow through woman, not to be dammed up and forced into new and twisted channels. Persea gave Thyestes a prophecy so that his weakened mind had something to hold on to, and yet she is still a priestess and she may have spoken truly but not for herself nor for him."

I thought of the High King's words again, but I was too weary now to make them come clear in my own mind. I did not see how alone the two kingdoms could survive an attack from Mycenae, or when it would come, but it was further away from me now than my next night's sleep.

We sat for a little while without speaking on the rim of the pool, then Chryseis said, "If she's killed Philon too. . . ."

"Philon's at Mycenae."

"Oh no!"

"I saw him this morning. I don't know how or why, but he was in the crowd outside the citadel as we were driven away."

"How could a small boy get so far?"

"Your women may be able to pass almost unnoticed, but if anyone's better at being inconspicuous, then it's a child. No one will notice and stop a small boy who seems to know where he's going. Did he know about Diomedes?"

"Yes, I suppose he must have done. The first of the survivors got back late yesterday evening. There was no certain news but they thought that he might have been taken."

"Then that's where Philon's gone. I wonder if he can stay alive till the new moon. I wonder if Diomedes can."

Chryseis drew closer to me. It was still hot and airless even though the night had fallen, and my fever was coming back—my whole body ached.

"He won't come for your watching, my dear," she said. "Go back to Leander and lie across his doorway if you must, but there's nothing else you can do."

I stood up slowly. "Not tonight, nor any of the nights till the end, but when that comes I shall kill two Myceneans for Damon, and two for myself, and then two for Diomedes. After that I shall ride to Mycenae with the cloak and armour he must wear when we bring him home."

"Six deaths, Hipponax? How if you aren't there to greet Diomedes after all?"

"Chryseis, I'm not boasting and I hope I'm not being a fool, but you can't know how I felt yesterday in the east valley,

125

lying ill behind a rock while my brother died and our men were scattered. I know that if I had had ten spears in ten hands it would have made very little difference, but when our day comes, just for once I shall be Hipponax the warrior again, to wash the sour taste from my mouth."

"I didn't think that you were a warlike man," she said. "No, I don't mean that you're a coward, I know you're not."

I took both her hands in mine and peered down into the small face where the great dark eyes shone. "Some men fight for no reason, some when the reason is good and then with joy, some only when there is no other way. That's how I am, Chryseis, but if ever I'm to take you home to a house unburned and orchards green above unhacked roots, then once I must find joy in battle, and I think this time I won't have far to look for it."

Three days passed. Now a south wind blew unseasonably from the sea, though it brought no coolness with it as it scoured the parched, golden fields of Argos. The sun was overcast, yet even under the portico where Leander lay there seemed no protection from its sullen glare. My fever had gone but he still lay propped up with pillows, chained to a bed by his injured leg. In three days more it would be the new moon.

Since the confining of Persea, there had been little that Leander could do at Argos, but there was little that he could do anywhere, and he had remained with us rather than go home to Tiryns. It was near Argos that the battle would take place, and to Argos that Agamemnon would come, if he ever came. For the moment, sick and disheartened as he was, Leander ruled in the citadel, while men guessed in whispers what would happen to Diomedes if help did not come in time.

All that could be done to prepare for the battle had gone on around us under the orders of Mecistheos, and the steward of Tiryns had reported all in readiness there. Now Kaletor

126

watched the northern borders and Leander spent the days of his recovery in a state of heartbreaking patience, controlling the pain in his mind as well as in his body with the fortitude of a man. He had grown up in a hard school and there was much that he could teach me.

I was sitting on a stool beside his couch, tired in the heat, staring at nothing, and when Leander touched my shoulder I jumped, because I had been lost in the dark place in my mind, worrying at it like a child with a sore finger.

"Hipponax, don't! Can't you be still, knowing that there's nothing you can do?"

"That's why it hurts so much; that—and knowing what it's really like in Mycenae."

"That makes it worse?"

"Of course it does. Diomedes' mother died when he was a baby, but I suppose I worry about him the way she would, only no woman when she sends her boy out to fight really knows what it's going to be like. She imagines it as bad, she can't see how bad. If I'd never seen Diomedes after he'd been captured, I wouldn't know what he looked like as a prisoner. I've seen him dirty and weary or hurt after a fall a thousand times; that was different. I would help him to clean up and in the morning he was all right. Where he is now there isn't any morning; I know how the foul air hangs in that prison, how the body aches for somewhere to rest, and how the hours hardly seem to be passing at all."

"Diomedes is strong, he'll come through it. There may be only three more days."

"I've only been the king's cupbearer for a few days. For seven years before that Diomedes grew up in my father's house and when I asked him to do a thing he did it. I can't take that seven years away from my life even though they're over now. They changed me as much as they changed him, and the habit of caring for his well-being is too deep a part of me now to be easily quieted when he's suffering. Is that unnatural?"

I turned to look at Leander. "No," he said, "only unfamiliar. I'm probably heartless because I've learned to shut my mind off from things I can't alter, because that's the only way I can be a king."

We were silent then for a while. Leander lay back against the pillows, shifting restlessly.

"One more day, and then whether this leg will hold me or not, the last decisions must be made and I must be able to stand in my chariot. Achates has been gone seven days now. If there's no word from him before dawn I think I shall begin to lose hope."

A ray of yellow light shone briefly across the courtyard as the sun dropped below the bank of cloud above the western mountains; it faded and the quick summer dark flowed down around us. The wind, which had slackened as twilight came, blew even more strongly out of the starless sky as the great citadel, reared on its hilltop above the town, settled for the night. Torches flared above the wall from the shelter of the guardrooms, a shutter, blown back on its hinges, clattered against the wall; the saffron curtains in Leander's sleeping room blew out and eddied in the draught which was still stale and warm.

I helped Leander's squire prepare him for bed. It was still early but he was glad to rest while he could. Although the aching weariness of the first days was gone, his leg kept him awake at night. We bandaged it with cool, herb-soaked dressings while he looked on ruefully.

"It's only stiff, my lord, because you haven't been able to use it," said the squire. "Now the wound is healing and it's not so swollen, you should feel a difference."

"Yes, I suppose so. Tomorrow I must try it out with more than a few steps round this room. What's that?"

Horns were blowing down by the main gate, steps ran past the door, and there was a distant shout.

The squire went to the window, but it faced north, away from the main approach to the citadel. I threw open the door. The guards were looking down the gallery, spears ready, straining to hear.

"Go and see what it is," Leander called to his servant.

The young man ran off. Leander had thrown back the bed-covers and was easing his stiff leg over the side of the bed.

"I don't care if it's good news or bad, but I'm not receiving it lying here naked."

I helped to put a robe of red wool round his thin, scarred body, and he limped over to a carved chair. The squire had not come back, and now the noise was inside the palace, close below us. I went to the doorway again. The passage past the sleeping rooms was very dim. Suddenly a blaze of light shone at the far end where the stairway went down towards the great hall; two torchbearers came round the corner and after them Mecistheos, turning aside to speak to a man who walked behind him. The press of faces further back was blurred by the wavering light, but I was only looking at the tall stranger who strode towards me.

Leander behind called, "Hipponax, for pity's sake who is it?"

"Agamemnon!" The name itself was a battle cry.

I stepped back behind Leander's chair, the guard outside brought their spears to a salute, and Mecistheos stood aside to let the son of Atreus come first into the room.

This is how a High King should look, I thought, bowing low before the tall man in the travel-stained cloak. He was between thirty and forty years old, strong, yet not heavily built, with a big face very wide between the eyes, and a powerful jaw under his thick, black beard. Leander pushed himself

upright, still holding on to the arms of his chair. I took a half step forward to help him, and then realized that I was not needed as he stood looking up at the dark man who seemed already to be a king.

Agamemnon strode forward and took him by the shoulders in a gracious gesture that was part greeting and part support.

"Leander of Tiryns!" He seemed to like what he saw.

"Agamemnon, you came." Leander's voice broke, and he dropped his eyes for a moment. "The king of Tiryns greets the High King of Mycenae."

Agamemnon pushed him gently back into his chair. "I shall not forget that you were the first to call me that."

"I did so in the name of Argos and Diomedes, who would greet you by that name himself if he were here."

Achates and our own captain, worn but triumphant, had followed Agamemnon into the room and closed the door firmly on those others who would have liked to come in after them. Mecistheos drew forward another chair and Leander turned to me.

"Wine, Hipponax."

Two gold cups stood on a table near the bed, beside a slender-necked wine jug. I drew water from the pottery cooler and mixed the crimson liquid. The two kings paused, the cups in their hands, to pour a few drops in libation, and then drank deep. By the time I had taken wine to the other men in the room they were seated facing each other; Leander's face was flushed and more alive than I had ever seen it. I saw how much he must have felt the burden of being older than Diomedes; now at last there was another king in Argos.

He raised his hands and let them fall in his lap, almost wordless before the large, smiling man. "But how is it that you came so soon, and without word reaching me from the frontier guards?"

"How could they send news they did not know? I didn't come across the passes from Sparta, I came by sea."

"By sea? But I don't understand. It's three times as far round the coast as overland."

"King Leander, let me tell you how it happened. By good fortune I was at home when your emissaries reached the palace, and they had made good time. I suppose that I've dreamed for years of a messsge out of Mycenae that would bring me home, and it's as well that I did, for I knew the voice of the Gods when it came and I knew what I must do. If my plans hadn't been half prepared I don't think I could have travelled so swiftly. When the day comes it's like lightning out of a clear sky." He paused.

"Yes," said Leander softly, "I know."

"Before our plans were finally made, while we were assembling the men I could bring—my own few, those my brother who will one day be king of Sparta could lend me—word came that Thyestes had closed the passes. Then I knew that if we must cut our way to Argos we should come too late, and if the Gods did not speak again we were lost. But they did."

"A wind from the south?"

"Yes, but that was later. Word came up to the palace, this time from the coast, that eight ships which had been trading west to Pylos had come into the harbour. With those that we had already there were enough. Then I sacrificed to the Sea Warden and his daughters, and though the winds were still changeable the omens were good and we set sail. If the wind had blown from the south one day earlier we should never have rounded Cape Malia—the last of the ships was barely clear when it changed. All last night we sailed with bare masts, and today the ships have flown through the waves faster than birds can fly. A little before sunset we drew near the bay of Argos and sheltered behind the last headland, waiting for the dark. I knew that Thyestes could have no idea yet that we were so near, and I thought surprise might give us the one extra advantage we need. The ships are beached well hidden from Mycenean eyes, and by dawn my men will be safe in the olive groves below the town."

"How many could you bring?"

"Six hundreds, but no horses, though we have chariots and men trained to use them if you have teams to spare."

Leander turned to the two envoys. "I can't find words to thank you now, but when Argos is safe and Diomedes free you shall be rewarded. Lord Agamemnon, the wind has blown you with little rest these last nights. There are still three days to the new moon. In the morning we can make our plans."

"Three days; will your leg bear you in two, do you think?"

"If it must."

"Then, Leander, rest while you can, because I think that for too long you have been forced to fight to the direction of your enemy, and I think that even before the moon changes it may be that Thyestes will hear knocking at his gate."

13

THE RIDERLESS CHARIOT

WIND blowing through the reed beds told me where the river lay during the hours of darkness. The jerk as my head fell forward woke me from the last of many dozes, and this time I could see the line of tossing flowerheads against the first grey in the eastern sky. There was a stirring on either side in the half-light as the men sat up and felt for their weapons, knowing that dawn was near.

The leather straps creaked as Leander shifted his position on the floor of the chariot, and the horses snuffled and moved their feet, feeling the change in the wind.

I looked up at the paling sky. "Kaletor will be moving his men forward soon now. I hope Agamemnon across the river is ready. How long, do you think, till the Myceneans reach us?"

"I don't know," said Leander. "It's hard to tell how time will go in a battle, and our plan isn't a simple one; but we should hear them coming!"

I heard Achates laugh, back in the shadows. "I wish I was a hawk, high up, to see from the sky how they look running out of the trees and towards our spear points."

"And to see their full strength, where the weak places are, so Agamemnon may know where to strike. Yes, it would be useful, but only the Gods see us like that—small and quarrelsome as ants."

The wind tugged at Leander's hair and blew wisps of grass

around the wheels of the chariot. I sat on, frozen into the discomfort of a wakeful night, stiff and a little cold, with a bitter taste in my mouth, not ready yet to get up and let some exercise bring the life back into my body. Now the men were all awake, sitting in quiet groups, facing the east. A squire came up from the wagons in the rear with bread and a jug of wine. Leander drank and gave it to Achates.

"Pass the word down for the men to eat while they can, and see that their captains repeat their orders to them again. This isn't a battle when I can ride along the line waving a spear and crying 'victory', and they must be very sure how we expect the fighting to go and what they are to do."

Achates bowed and strode away. I got up at last and went to my horses' heads, checking their harness piece by piece, and every part of the chariot, although this time I had a man to do it for me. A bundle was stowed away where it would not interfere with our legs—the armour of Diomedes.

I came back to Leander as he was pulling himself up to try his full weight on the right leg. It seemed to bear. "Good," he said. "I didn't want to be strapped upright to go into battle, but leg or no leg, when the chariots advance I'm going to lead them."

I understood how he felt, though I wondered how he was going to do it, for it is the braced right leg that holds a man steady in a chariot. His mind had the thoughts in it that had been in my own when I had spoken to Chryseis in the courtyard of the women; only victory could wipe out the humiliation before Thyestes at Mycenae. The band of gold above the eastern mountains was spreading up the sky, the wind dropped for a moment and I strained my ears, but all was still quiet under the trees at the top of the slope on the other side of the river.

I picked up my helmet, shook out the long plume, and fastened the straps under my chin. A heartbeat ago I had not

135

been frightened, now my stomach was twisting in the sickeningly familiar way against my backbone and I felt cold above the eyes. I bent forward, adjusting my leg guards, and wiped the beading of sweat from my upper lip. Then I heard a man's voice singing softly, quite close. It was Achates, stringing his great bow of wood and horn. I heard a familiar name.

"What's that?" I asked.

"What?"

"The song you were singing."

"I don't know. No, wait a minute. I hadn't realized that I was, but it's a habit I have before any danger, so it must have been a sad song, I find it makes me fight better. Now what was it, I know, it must have been the thought of Diomedes put it into my mind."

He kept his voice low but clear, marking time against his shield with one hand:

"*Tydeos shone like a god, as he leapt on the host of the Thebans,*
But the flesh of a man is mortal and his life is a thing soon done.
Boreas, wind from the north, fly back from the city of Kadmos,
Tell of the heroes who ride, safe homeward in honour.

The wind from the north is keen, and cuts down hope like a knifeblade.
'*Seven there came against Thebes, now her gates hang open,*
And men heap mounds for the dead who fell in the battle,
A tomb for each prince, and 'neath Thebes' walls there are seven.'"

"Hush," I said, "and may our south wind avert the omen. How can sorrow like that make you fight better?"

"I don't know, but each of us carries some charm in his

136

mind that he uses to make him strong for battle. That's mine, and I shall fight all the better by your side for having sung it. I think you have your own too."

"I only need one thing to make me fight," I said bitterly, and prodded the bundle in my chariot wrapped in Diomedes' cloak. "Do you think we shall be in time, Achates?"

"Put it this way. I think with any other plan we would have been too late."

"Fighting when Thyestes expected us, lined up in a row for his chariots to cut to pieces when he chose? Yes, I suppose so. The Cretan would have hanged Diomedes from the walls of the citadel, and us after him."

"Listen," he said, turning back towards the river.

"No, it's only the wind. Kaletor's men have to move forward to attack the enemy camp, and then fall back but not too quickly. We won't hear them yet."

"Chariots! If only we'd had enough for a pitched battle. Three chariots are worth a hundred foot soldiers."

"We were without chariots in the east valley," I reminded him. "It's a lesson you only have to be taught once, but Agamemnon's plan was quite plain, and I don't see what else we could have done. We have to bring the enemy down out of the woods and then cut the two roads behind them with what mounted men we've got, so that none of their reinforcements can get through to them, and no accurate word come to the citadel. Then Agamemnon on the other bank and we on this can roll them up like an old cloak between us."

Leander came halting back down the line, leaning on the arm of his squire. "You're ready, Hipponax? You know what you must do?"

"Yes, my lord. Leave the main fighting to Agamemnon and follow you up to the citadel."

All along the waiting line there was a ripple as men paused and turned, listening.

"It's begun," said Leander. "Get the men as much out of sight as possible."

Achates settled the strung bow over his shoulder, clasped my hand, and turned back to his chariot further down the line.

The groups around us broke up and disolved as the foot soldiers disappeared into the low thickets that ran part way across the pasture where we were waiting. The few chariots on the right wheeled for the partial cover of the reed beds. At least the first Myceneans to cross the river would have no accurate idea of our strength, would not see at once that they were being led forward into a trap as delicately as one line of dancers retires as another advances.

It was daylight now except for the colour that only the sun would bring. A running man broke through the bushes on the far side of the river and stumbled through the places where the water still ran wide and shallow among the sandbanks, pausing to look along our line for Leander. The young king bent forward from his chariot to hear his message.

"Kaletor's men are falling back, Lord King, and the enemy are following. Some of them haven't even bothered to arm properly. But as I left the general there were chariots on the road to Mycenae and they weren't ours."

Leander looked quickly across at me, and then called back to the captains, "Steady, wait for my signal."

The first of our men came from the trees, turned back to fight again, and then ran on towards the river bank. They were picked men, for any warrior who has fought for his life knows that it can be more difficult to retreat in order than to advance. They were still some way off, small, remote figures. I stood, my hand close to the spear holder on my chariot's rim, watching the place directly opposite where a willow grew alone, its roots almost in the water. The men I was about to kill would cross there.

The first Myceneans reached the river as the sun's eye leaped above the mountains and the air turned gold. There were no horses, only running men, the flashing of bronze, and a wave of noise that was suddenly very close. I looked quickly sideways again at Leander. The Myceneans had seen our thin line of chariots by now and paused, then with a roar they ran down across the shingle and through the water, throwing up plumes of spray to dance fire-coloured in the sun. My charioteer bent low over the reins, his hand on the whip.

Now all our rearguard were across the river, the ground back up to the trees was thick with men, and the first chariots were clattering down the road that ran to the ford. Still Leander held our men back. The first of the enemy checked uncertainly at the crumbling edge of the river bank, then the numbers behind them pressed them on, straight towards us.

"Forward!" Leander's war-cry carried almost as Diomedes' had done. There was no time to look back, but I heard an answering cry from the foot soldiers behind us as they rose from the ground and charged. The first rank of the enemy stopped again, confused; a few spears flew, but their chariots were still beyond the river.

My charioteer bent low behind my shield as we ploughed into them. "They're sheep," he shouted. "Let's drive them home."

I thought for one instant of my boast to Chryseis, and my strength grew greater than the fear all men have before their first blow has been struck. I drove for the willow, where the thickest tangle of Myceneans was clambering with difficulty up the steep ground. There was no room for spear work, I stabbed down with my short sword at helmeted heads, balancing for the tug and thrust as the bronze point met leather and flesh. The chariot swayed as a cluster of men, half-seen out of the corner of my eye, charged on the other side and the charioteer dragged on the reins till the horses, slewing round in the churned-up wheel marks, struck out with their murderous hooves, screaming in anger.

I was hot now, with sweat running into my eyes. A dagger stabbed up past the side of the chariot and gashed my leg, but the man who held it jumped clear. There was no time to count wounds or deaths, this was fighting without thought; if my arm and eye were quick enough I should live, if not—others already lay dead.

There was clear ground all round the chariot except for the scarlet tangle between the horses' hooves. We swung left towards Leander. His team were right down in the water, the wheels clogged in a patch of sand, the horses plunging. All down the line the fighting still seemed to be close to the river. The Myceneans had not broken through.

"Go round," I shouted to my man. "It's too steep to go down here." Then I jumped into the shallow water and waded towards Leander.

His driver was slumped over the side with blood running from below his breastplate. There was barely room behind him on the shifting platform, but I leant far forward to catch at the trailing reins, and steady the frightened horses.

As I got the chariot back on to firmer ground, bending almost double for Leander to thrust across my back at the splashing shouting enemy, our men closed around us, and Achates was there, helping to drag the wounded man free.

"I'll drive," he shouted. "Look, they're breaking towards the trees."

I leapt down to make room for him and looked across the river. Most of the Myceneans were weaving uncertainly on the far side, and some were already trailing back across the open ground below the trees.

"Sound the horns!" shouted Leander.

They brayed to our right, and then much further away, an answer from the cornland on the far side. The Myceneans heard them too; I saw two of their captains shout to the men, trying to form a line to face the new danger.

Then Achates pointed. "Look, under the trees!" There were more men coming out into the sun, meeting the fugitives and sending them back; and beyond them more chariots came down the road from Mycenae. Both armies turned and paused as they rolled out into the meadow, fresh and unmarked by battle.

"Agamemnon?" I called.

"No, the guard of Thyestes; see his colours. The Cretan has brought down reinforcements from the citadel. Agamemnon hasn't been able to cut the road after all."

The first men of our right wing came running up the far bank of the river, then hesitated, for the fighting seemed to have stopped, with the flat banks of gravel forming the boundary between the two armies. All eyes were on the chariots rolling down from the eastern road.

"Why doesn't Agamemnon attack?" my charioteer asked.

"Look, they're sending out a herald."

One of the teams had broken away from the others and was coming straight towards the water's edge, while the man in it held the wand of a herald high. Gelanor rode down into the water to meet him.

"No further," he called. "Speak from where you are so we can all hear you."

The herald reined in his team and it became very quiet, with only the small water noises and the frightened crying of the river birds which had been wheeling and swooping above the heads of the fighting men.

"Captains of Argos!" he shouted. "Unless there is some king among you. Have you had your fill of being killed, or shall we send your own lord back to you to strengthen you for the fight?" He swung his arm back, pointing up the hill.

It was not far to where the main body of the chariots had

been halted, and the men around the horses could be clearly seen. As our eyes followed the pointing hand they parted to show a huddle of prisoners, each held between two guards. Even at this distance they looked miserably weak, almost naked. The blood pounded behind my eyes, almost blinding me, as I saw first the red head of Ion, then Diomedes, a little ahead of the others.

"We see your prisoners," shouted Leander. "Now make your message clearer, if you are indeed a herald."

A guard tugged at a rope and Diomedes fell forward on to his knees, so I knew that his hands were tied. The leading chariot rolled clear of the Myceneans who were moving round it.

"You shall have your king of Argos if he can run as fast as our horses," called the herald, and laughed.

They were tying the rope that bound Diomedes to the chariot axle; he would lose his footing at once and be broken on the rough ground in the charge to the river, if he should live that far. I did not know that I was shouting till Achates pushed my driver to one side and seized me, one arm round my body, a hand over my mouth.

"Be silent! Would you have him die sooner than he need?"

A new voice, Agamemnon's, came from across the water. "And what would save the life of King Diomedes and his companions?"

"Withdraw all your men back to Argos and wait there for the High King's commands."

Achates was cursing low but fluently. "To die by the sword is one thing, but like that among the mud and stones . . . may the Mistress blast them!"

The wind blew among the reeds, a horse neighed, there was a clink of armour. I could feel that the sun was already very hot, but my body was cold with the chilled sweat of the fighting drying on it. Leander turned his chariot to the right and drove it slantwise across the sandbanks towards Agamemnon, standing in the front rank of his men. He never reached him.

Back up the hillside there was the scream of a frightened horse, a howl of human pain, and the chariot seemed to break loose from the men around it and thunder down towards us. Achates' hand pushed up to cover my eyes, as I wrestled with him.

Then, "No, he's not there. Look."

I wrenched free, staring towards the galloping horses. Nothing bumped behind the chariot, and it seemed to be empty.

"But how? There's no one there and yet those horses are being driven," shouted Achates into my ear.

I saw a tuft of fair hair above the rim of the chariot. "Diomedes, Diomedes, the riderless chariot!" The release of all my terror and agony was in my voice.

I was drowned by the ringing of horns at both ends of our battle line as our men surged forward and down into the shallow strands of water, wheels thundering over the pebbles and spray churned high above the tossing heads of the horses as the foot soldiers ran on. Achates had caught the reins and I nearly fell as we jerked forward after them. The whole hillside above and east of the river seemed to be moving.

The single chariot crashed through the reeds and down into the water, but the horses plunged on. We were nearly beside them when a wheel broke loose, sending the chariot over on one side.

I jumped from the rail and ducked under the flailing hooves round to the lower side. Diomedes lay half in the water, partly pinned down. I slashed the reins free where they had tangled in the ropes that still held him, and got my arm beneath his body so that he would not slip further down into the stream. Achates was still above us in the chariot. Diomedes saw him and shouted, "Find Philon."

"Who?"

143

"He's a small boy, there can't be very many up there on the hill. Go quickly, Achates, he may be dead already."

The chariot lurched as the horses struggled to get a footing on the far bank, and then Achates had thundered up and on towards the battle.

14

THE OPENED GATES

I CUT the last of the ropes that tied Diomedes' wrists and he pulled himself up till he rested on the tilted floor of the chariot, head bent so that I could not yet see his face. I ran my arms quickly up his arms and legs; he was wet and covered with muck from the river but nothing seemed to be broken. Then he put his head down between his knees and was sick.

When it was over he stood up, with the water still splashing past his knees, and looked back at the hillside. We were too low to see much, but most of the shouting seemed to be further away. Diomedes looked at me then and his face split from a thin, strange mask to a ghost of his familiar smile.

"So Agamemnon came!"

"Yes, two nights ago."

"I never thought of that, it seemed too soon. When the guards came an hour ago I thought Thyestes was going to kill us after all, without waiting for the battle. And now this." He began to shiver.

There was no one now in the water, and only the baggage wagons on our side of the river. My chariot and Diomedes' armour with it was up the hillside, so I tried to turn him back to where the servants were tending the wounded among the trees.

"No." He pulled away. "I must go after Agamemnon and my men."

We climbed the bank, and I pulled off my cloak and wrapped it round him. One of our men lay twisting in the grass, a spear high up through his leg.

"Is it the king?" he gasped.

Diomedes dropped on his knees in the blood-drenched grass, but before he could answer, the man's staring eyes turned in his head and he was still. The fighting was so newly passed that the ground here was ugly with the awkward shapes of the dead, and those who still moved and cried. Further up a detail of our men were gathered round the prisoners. Diomedes saw them.

"So the others are safe. I didn't think there would be time to kill them all."

"But Diomedes, what happened?"

He looked at me, the tired eyes sunk deep beneath his brows. "Of course, you don't know. Wait, here's Achates."

The bowman was alone in the chariot as he halted it beside us.

"Did you find him? If he's dead . . ."

"No, he's hurt but he won't die. I left him with the wounded up there by the trees; he's been stunned by the kick from a horse."

Achates threw the reins to a man whose right hand was twisted inside his blood-stained tunic and jumped down. "King Diomedes, we must arm you, or you'll die even now from a stray spear. Then tell me who this boy is."

I stripped off the last of Diomedes' prison rags and rubbed him dry on my cloak while Achates untied the bundle of armour from inside the chariot. He stood patiently like a child while I pulled on the thin linen tunic that went beneath the padded body armour. Then he sat down so that I could fasten the metal-plated grieves while Achates gave him his sword.

Diomedes slung the scabbard over his shoulder and drew the blade part-way, looking down at it. "It was like my dream,

Hipponax," he said. "Something impossible to do and no strength left." He closed his eyes.

"Philon," I said. "Tell us how he was on the battlefield."

"I don't know how, but he was. I thought I saw him once before, pressed against the grating looking down into the prison, but it was dark and I might have dreamed it. It's difficult to keep the mind steady as the days pass."

"I know," I said. "But go on."

"When they brought us out this morning the citadel was in an uproar, it's been uncannily quiet the last two days, even to us. We were roped in twos and thrown into the chariots. I thought my back would be broken by the jolting, for the guards drove fast. When we came down past the trees I heard fighting but I couldn't guess what the Cretan was going to do. We stopped, and they pulled us out; I could see your chariots down by the river and so many men in our colours that I couldn't understand what was happening. It was when they re-tied our hands and pulled us forward that I saw Philon."

"How did he come to be among the soldiers?"

"I can't think, but you know how it is with horses. They don't wait still like men in tidy lines. They always shift around pulling the chariots about so that they must be held and soothed. He must have got close up in the confusion. I saw him standing by the head of the lead horse, feeding him a handful of fresh grass. After that I understood what they were going to do to me, and I lost sight of him while I was being tied to the chariot."

He stopped and dropped his head again. Achates gripped his shoulder, but I could not move or speak yet, it was still too close. Horns sounded up in the orchards and he looked up quickly. Men were still fighting beneath the trees, and Agamemnon's bodyguard were running up from the broken ground on the east bank of the river.

"I remember looking at the wooden frame of the chariot

floor," said Diomedes, "and thinking that if I could get a knee up and hold on, I might be all right. But I knew the driver would kick me back on to the ground if he could. The reins hung ready, looped over the side and on to the floor. Then I saw Philon again; he came out under the horses' bellies. All the guards were looking down towards the heralds, I could guess what they were saying but I hadn't time to listen because Philon looked me straight in the eyes and opened one of his hands so that I could see he was holding a long, straight thorn. All at the same moment the man who was holding me bent forward to measure the rope, Philon slashed up at the offside horse's belly, and I jumped forward towards that loop of reins. I got hold of it but the rope caught somewhere and I couldn't have stood upright even if it had been safe to, but the sides of the chariot were lattice-work and I steered downhill. I've never felt anything so wonderful as when the water splashed up on my bare skin. Achates, you're sure that Philon's all right?"

"Yes, King Diomedes. I saw him myself."

"Hipponax, do you remember the last day at Dimini before Mecistheos came for me, the day that I fell out of the chariot? You were cross then, but I think I learnt that one lesson."

I turned away to pick up his helmet. This was not a time when I wanted Diomedes to see me weep. One of Agamemnon's captains came running across the hillside.

"The Myceneans have broken, my lord. The High King is riding for the citadel, and your men have the enemy cornered up where the three roads meet."

Leander's chariot, with his helmet crest blowing above it like a yellow flame, came charging down the track. It seemed that the wounded leg was lasting well, for Leander stood easily poised above the bronze-trimmed rail, his eyes blazing. The wheels stopped in a flurry of small stones. Diomedes put

a hand on the rim to jump up beside him; then he swayed as if he was going to faint.

I steadied him as Leander bent over, holding him by the shoulders.

"Can you ride, Diomedes? I don't want to go on to Mycenae without you."

"Mycenae? Hipponax, give me something to drink and I'll manage."

I gave him water mixed with wine, from the leather bottle in Leander's chariot. He rubbed his hands over his face, settled the helmet strap under his chin, and levered himself off from the side of the chariot.

"That's better, now for the citadel of the lions . . . again."

We passed the first of our men at the edge of the trees. Ahead, a handful of Myceneans still fought around an upturned chariot. We cut through them and then Leander held back to let us go ahead, for the road was not wide enough for two teams abreast.

Since the empty chariot had clattered down the hillside I had not been part of the main battle, now I was glad of a last chance to strike at Mycenean helmets and remember Thyestes and his Cretan captain.

We crashed through the last of the enemy's rearguard and they turned to run up among the trees where our men were hunting them. Diomedes bent far out to thrust with the long bronze flame of his sword. Then the road was empty ahead.

I realized that since we had left the river the morning light, which should have been growing stronger, was fading away. I looked up at the sky. The wind had dropped for a moment but the sun was lost behind a small dark cloud. Then Diomedes pointed back towards the south as we climbed higher up from the plain. The sky over the sea boiled black as evening with dark cloud, and great towers of white-flecked murk were rushing in over the land. As the horses slowed for a bend, lightning flashed back down the valley and the first thunder sounded louder than the drumming of our wheels.

"The Gods are riding with us!" shouted Diomedes, his mouth against my ear.

The thunder pealed again nearer, over Argos, and the olives beside the road bent in the beginning of the storm wind; a flurry of small birds flew low in front of the horses, calling shrilly. I looked ahead; Mycenae still rode high on its spike of rock in the last of the sun, but the twin mountains behind were black, their summits already engulfed in the advancing sea of cloud.

The rain hit us like a storm at sea, a black line running across the barley stubble. The horses shied and then galloped on, heads down; almost at once their backs were darkened with water and their wet manes blew out like tangled seaweed.

Rain ran down my face, plastered my dripping cloak against my legs and trickled beneath my armour; the reins slipped in my cold fingers.

Diomedes beside me was singing, his face held up to the rain as if it was pouring life back into him the way the first showers do to a parched field. The thunder was almost continuous and I could not hear the words. A sheet of blue lightning crackled over us and I reined back, looking behind at Leander to see if we should go on, but he was shouting to Achates and their pace had not slackened.

The road up to the citadel was now a river, with small stones, sticks and the dry leaves from beneath the olives swept down among the horses' hooves. We had caught up with Agamemnon's men and the hillside under the trees was covered with figures running, heads down, into the storm. Rounding the last turn before the citadel we could see the road up as far as the gate; it was almost choked with chariots, mostly our own, but a few of them Mycenean, left broken beside the track. Far ahead, almost below the walls, was one of our own, and a flash even through the storm darkness of bronze armour—Agamemnon.

"He's in spear range from the walls," Diomedes shouted.

But the walls seemed to be unmanned. The teams ahead of us drove off into the rough ground on either side so that we could get through, and we were not far behind the High King as he approached the great gateway.

It was open, a dark mouth between the sloping walls, and the great lions, snarling still, were painted black with the rain. No voice challenged Agamemnon as he drew up before the citadel, no guard moved on the walls above the gatehouse. The space within the outer walls was clogged with damaged chariots, wounded men, horses loosed and not taken to the stables, with no captain to give any orders. There was a strange hush, as if uproar had been cut off short, except for the sobbing of a wounded man, out of sight behind the piles of sodden baggage.

The thunder rumbled again, a little further off, and the rain began to slacken, so that the wreck of Thyestes' army looked like the flotsam of some storm at sea, swept beyond the tide line. Still no one barred our path; Agamemnon seized the whip from his squire, called his panting horses to one last effort, and his war-cry echoed under the archway as he galloped up through the second gate and the slope beyond that led to the inner courtyard of the palace.

We followed him, our men crowding close behind. There were Myceneans here too but they were the palace people, slaves and attendants and a few women, drawn back into the corners, their hands empty. The great stairway to the hall that I had climbed in chains seven days before was bare, no captain with his men drawn up in line barred the way.

Agamemnon jumped down from his chariot and looked around him, a drawn sword still in his hand. The rain had almost ceased, pattering into the pools among the uneven stones. He ran lightly up the steps to the portico while Diomedes was dismounting stiffly, and stood at the top looking back into the courtyard where his own men were spilling up under the archway and along the walls, then out over the pale rain-washed country to the gleam of the sea.

The rest of us climbed the steps together till Diomedes paused half-way to turn and point among the western hills to where Dimini lay; so it was I who reached the High King first. He was waiting, smiling down at the young men below, his hands outstretched in welcome.

A shadow moved between the painted pillars, and my round shield slipped from its shoulder sling and into my left hand almost by itself. As the spear hissed out of the darkness my arm came up and I leapt sideways behind Agamemnon's back. The force of the blow threw me off my feet, with the shield split half across and the spear trailing. Then the young kings and Achates ran past me as I knelt bowed over an arm deeply grazed by the spear head where it had struck me through the triple thickness of leather.

Swords clashed within the hall, I slid the damaged shield from my arm and ran after Diomedes.

The shutters were closed above on two sides of the upper galleries to keep out the rain, and in the half darkness below, the kings of Argos and Tiryns were stalking their prey. It was the Cretan, partly armed, his bronze breastplate askew above the turquoise kilt, bareheaded with the long oiled curls in a blood-matted tangle round his face.

He was light on his feet as a cat, and as silent. Diomedes and Leander were working him together like a couple of hounds, forcing him pace by pace out into the lighter corner near the royal seat. I saw Achates move in the shadows, edging behind him, then he stumbled over a stool and kicked it away clattering across the polished floor. Leander checked at the sound and the Cretan leapt back into the shadows.

I pulled the embroidered cover off a table and twisted it around my arm; the blood still came through, but more slowly. I was beginning to feel the pain which had been hidden before in the numbness of the blow. Agamemnon's sword flashed beside me.

"My lord," I whispered, "leave them. This is an old quarrel."

There was no sound in the hall then except for the heavy breathing of the hunted man and Leander's dragging tread. Achates had been edging sideways again in the gloom. Suddenly his voice came very loud, "So ha!"

The Cretan jumped, his foot slipped in the pool of water beneath an open shutter, he glanced half round, judging the distance behind him to the steps of the royal dais, missed his footing and went backwards up them. Diomedes' sword flickered as the blade went in beneath the loosened buckles below the left arm. It was one clean thrust, and enough, although Leander was ready. The Cretan twisted, slipping loose from the blade, grasping the king's chair even as I had seen Thyestes do before, only this time there was no one to hold him and he crashed down to lie where we had knelt on the day when his lord had called for kings from among the prisoners at his feet.

Diomedes looked thoughtfully at the blood on his sword and then bent to wipe it clean on the edge of the man's kilt. A scarlet stain was spreading slowly across the crimson octopus I had seen before; then Diomedes turned and spoke very solemnly to Agamemnon.

"Argos greets the High King; your hall is clean now for you to enter."

I waited, leaning against the parapet of the gallery above the great hall, tightening the knots of a makeshift bandage about my throbbing arm. Men with drawn swords prowled along passages that led to the royal sleeping rooms, but the strange hush still hung over the citadel; this was not a captured palace to be sacked. Achates called from a corner to the left.

"Lord Agamemnon."

He strode past me as Diomedes came up the stairs. "Which way?"

I pointed, wordless. He ran towards the open door and after Agamemnon into the room. Achates stood in the threshold across the sprawled body of what must have been the last loyal guard in the palace. I looked past him into the half-darkness beyond; there were flapping hangings and a sour stuffy smell. I saw the corner of a disordered bed, with a purple blanket half on the floor and the sheet stained with patches of green; there was a slow gasping noise, irregular and difficult.

"Is it Thyestes? Has he been hurt?"

"Not by us. I understand now—the broken defence and the open gates. The man there is so near death that it would be pride before the Gods to kill him before the moment they have chosen."

"I saw it in his face the day we were brought before him in the hall, but I didn't know it was so close. Is there no one with him?"

"Only two old women, if there's any comfort in them. The Gods know that he was cruel, but it's a bad death he has there at the end of a defeated life, and one I would wish on no one."

Diomedes came out sheathing his sword, then Agamemnon. They were both silent. Down in the great hall I found wine and water beside the great mixing bowl. Before he would drink Agamemnon poured water over his hands and emptied his full goblet before the hearth.

"To the Mistress. Before dusk every altar in the citadel shall smoke to her. Will you stay and feast with me, my lords of Argos and Tiryns?"

Leander and Diomedes looked at each other and then at the High King. The body of the Cretan had gone, though the stain of blood had not yet been washed from the plaster floor. Leander pointed to it.

"Tonight you will eat for the first time in your own hall, but not yet with quite the solemnity you would wish to keep among your guests. While the altars are smoking there are still many dark places in Mycenae that need to be made clean; I have just come from your prisons, my lord."

Agamemnon nodded, his face grave again. "Yes, I spoke without thinking. There's much for me to do here and you have duties yourselves that have waited too long at home. There is only one place where we shall each know peace tonight, and that is among our own people. When the moon is full we will feast."

15

THE SONG OF ACHATES

PHILON had been brought back from the battlefield to a little room near the apartments of the king. Chryseis cried when she saw him, after his body had been washed clean and the wound on his head dressed; he looked so small and it was clear there had been more kicks than food to be picked up in the citadel of Mycenae in the last days. He was sleepy and his head ached, but we fed and settled him between clean sheets in the finest bed he had ever lain in.

"Lie still now and go to sleep," said Chryseis. "I'm going to stay here where you can see me, and I won't go away even if you shut your eyes."

"You promise?" Philon lay relaxed against the pillows, but the hand that held hers was still gripping very tightly.

"Yes, now hush."

"But I want to see the king."

"He'll come when he can," I said. "But there are other things he must do first."

"Not any longer," said Diomedes from the doorway. He limped across the room, his helmet trailing from one hand. "Philon, how did you think of the thorn?"

"Didn't you ever see the boys down in the market upsetting the pack donkeys?"

"No, but I'm glad you did."

The child's eyelids dropped. "Tell me in the morning everything else that happened," said Diomedes. "We're both tired now. Sleep secure, all Argos is guarding you, just as you guarded me."

"I can stay here, can't I? You won't ever send me away somewhere else to grow up?"

"No, Philon. Not unless you choose to go away."

"Never. . . ." He was asleep even before we were out of the room.

I paused in the doorway to say goodnight to Chryseis and then followed Diomedes to his own room. He lay across the bed already asleep, his helmet, corselet and cloak dropped where they had fallen in a trail across the floor. I called the servant quietly and between us we undid his belt, slipped off the laced boots and drew up the cover. Nothing was as important tonight as sleep.

Then the man helped me to undress myself and rebound the awkward left arm. I did not notice at the time the respect with which he did it, turning down the cover on the small bed in the alcove near the door where I had slept on the nights since we came to the palace, and blowing out the lamps except for the one near Diomedes' bed.

When he had gone I did not lie down at once, for my weariness was of a different kind from that of Diomedes, and my wound was troubling me too much to make the possibility of sleep coming quickly very likely. I stood looking out of the window over the dark plain; the stars shone faintly among the last of the storm clouds, but there was no moon.

Diomedes sighed and turned over. I looked down at him and saw that he had been crying in his sleep; I did not think the memory of prison would loose him as quickly as its walls had done, but he was a man now and would be able to bear it. We had buried the boy from Dimini in the valley beside my brother and now I could not see clearly whether my place was still to be by his side.

I lay down on my bed, watching the steady flame of the

lamp, for the night was very still. Now that we were at peace together in this quiet room, he was gone from my care further than he had ever been in the days of prison. Not from my heart, and yet I had learned that my heart could hold more than one person at the same time. It was too early yet to decide where my loyalty lay.

In the morning when he first woke Diomedes was very quiet, then as the truth of his freedom came fully to him he was a boy again, home from a disagreeable journey.

He yelled as the servants lowered him into the steaming herb-scented water in the bath tub, and it reached the sores on his legs and back.

I sat on a stool out of their way, cursing my bandages which would not let me help as they bathed and oiled him. Mycenae had left some marks that time and youth would not heal. The bruises would fade and some of the flesh would come back, but his first youthfulness was gone, and when I saw the sores on his back I knew that now he would share some scars with Leander that he would not lose. Perhaps later he would tell me why he had been beaten.

He came back into the sleeping room swathed in towels and smelling of ointment and bath oil, his hair cut short. I could hear from the other room the servants exclaiming about what they had found in it and muttering that the bedcovers would have to be burnt.

"It's strange that everything in Argos is just as it was before we left for the east valley," he said. "I know that the fighting never came as far south as this, but so much has happened to me that I can't believe my clothes are still where I left them."

"There may be no smoking buildings and unburied bodies here, but there's still a lot to do," I said. "Remember the Lady Persea."

"I do, but first I must talk to Agamemnon. She is a priestess even if she abused her powers most terribly, and I can't do what I'd like to her. However, what about her attendant, your cousin, Hipponax?"

I looked up quickly. "Chryseis?"

"Yes, of course. She no longer has any reason to stay at Argos and I think it's high time she was married and at home."

"My father is her guardian," and then I stopped, for a guard was bowing in the doorway.

"Bias of Dimini is in the great hall. He sends his duty to the king and asks that he may speak to his son."

Diomedes turned to me, suddenly grave. "I must see him soon, Hipponax, but not today. Go to him now."

I went quickly down the stairway from the upper gallery. My father sat on a polished settle where the morning light fell across the bright floor from the doorway. I did not see how much he was changed until he turned, hearing my footsteps. The man who stood up so stiffly was old, with bowed shoulders, and on his face the deep lines I remembered from my grandfather when he was close to death.

I bent to kiss his hand; then he embraced me, holding me in his great arms, before I could persuade him to sit down again, for I was still too sore for much of such treatment. I had always known he loved Damon, though not till then quite how much. It was not that he had ever cared for us unequally so much as that now I was here and Damon was not, and never would be.

He remembered to ask about Diomedes and to examine my own wounds, and then when I could bear the silence beneath the conversation no longer I said, "Father we buried Damon, he wasn't left for the enemy to find. We can bring him home when the tomb is ready."

"Hipponax, you were with him? I didn't know that."

"No, Father, I didn't see him die, but it wasn't very long after before we found him. It was a good place."

"The men are already opening the family burial shaft. I had

hoped . . . I had thought that we might find him. I want my son in Dimini, and the last things done for him. I want to see them done myself."

"It might not yet be safe over in the east valley. Some of Thyestes' men fell back that way."

"But if it is?"

"Then if Diomedes will give me leave we can ride today." That made him start a little; Diomedes the king was not yet real for him. "It's early yet, we could be back not long after nightfall."

I left him to go back to the king, thinking that Diomedes was right and it was indeed too soon for them to meet. The thought of the day's work that now lay in front of me was bringing back the mood of bitter uncertainty from the days before the battle, and I knew now that I too would not rest until I had seen again the place where my brother lay, and where I had wished I was dead with him. If I felt that, then how much more must it be in my father's mind?

We reached the valley after midday. It lay bare and silent in the heat except for the green place in the centre where the spring was. The goats had not yet been driven back to their pasture and in the eight days since the ambush nothing could have altered, and yet the spur of hillside where we had waited for the dawn, and the turn where I had hidden with Diomedes from the chariots did not look the same.

It had been even further round by the road but the going was better and we had made good time in spite of the wagon that my father's men drove behind us to take the body of the dead home. We stopped on the track above the spring, and I led my father down through the undergrowth towards the green bushes and the waterwashed pebbles. Here nothing had changed except that the poppies were faded above the vivid moss and the little daisies.

It was dark before we reached the river on our return, and

even later before the lights of the citadel were above us. My father reined in the horses and turned to me. It had been a long and silent journey.

"I must go with the dead," he said. "But Diomedes will need you."

"Send me word when the tomb is ready," I answered, as I embraced him. "Before, there wasn't time to weep for my brother."

He drove off slowly into the darkness and I climbed alone towards the postern gate of the palace. The guard passed me in and I walked wearily up through the passages and lower courtyards towards the portico of the great hall. It was a hot night, still after the storm of the day before, though the air smelled clean. Even here the song of the cicadas came up from the fields below the citadel.

Light flooded across the great courtyard from the open doors of the hall. I saw the helmeted guards in silhouette against it, and the squires and servants passing to and fro; there seemed to be more people about than I had expected. I heard laughter, and then a hush followed by the voice of a minstrel.

"Who is with the king?" I asked the captain at the door.

"Leander of Tiryns. Achates the bowman is singing for them."

I paused on the threshold. Achates was sitting in the bard's seat near the fire, while the lords of Argos feasted. Light from the central fire and four smaller braziers shone on the metal dishes that the squires carried from the serving tables, and the wine poured high from glazed jugs, while the serving maids followed the housekeeper, carrying baskets of bread and fruit.

They were all there, Mecistheos the tall and silent who had seen the comings and going of the kings and had held the citadel safe between his hands while they were away, whom no one remembered while we fought on the fringes of the kingdom but whose days had been as weary as any that we had passed there. Kaletor sat beside him, short legs stuck out in front of him, watching the captains and courtiers above the rim of a mighty drinking cup, ill at ease among the splendours of the palace. In the morning I knew he would be already riding far to the north, where men still fought among the furthest manors. As I watched him I thought that he would be glad to be gone, yet as his eyes rested on Diomedes I saw that he might be planning still another stage in the military education of his young king; like most educators he valued an apt pupil.

Now the laughter and the talk were hushed again for the singer, and watching Achates' face as he bent over the lyre, I wondered if he would not have been more at peace if he had been a bard and not a warrior, till I remembered the same thoughtful collectedness in his eyes as he had stalked the Cretan the day before. Then I began to listen to the song, and my heart jumped as I recognized the words he had sung on the battlefield by the river in yesterday's dawn.

"*Seven there came against Thebes, now her gates hang open,*
And men heap mounds for the dead who fell in the battle,
A tomb for each prince, and 'neath Thebes' walls there are
  seven.
Tydeos' bones are white in the earth of the northland,
But men spring up like flowers from the blood of the slain.
Diomedes, valiant in war, raise again your loud war-cry,
Let seven, the sons of the slain, again ride to Thebes,
To blot out the shame of the dead, and pour new blood on
  their ashes.
May the Mother of all men grant the prayers of her
  children."

A shout went up as Achates let his hands fall from the

strings, for though the song was familiar the ending was new.

"Diomedes!" shouted the men of Argos as I entered the hall, and I heard him laugh, as he thanked Achates, slipping a heavy bracelet from his arm to put into his hands. "But my lord, it is your own King Leander who is the valiant one, and the High King Agamemnon. I was a prisoner when the deeds were done that led to the victory."

"And who drove the riderless chariot down to the river, and who killed the Cretan?" asked Leander with his dry smile. "Diomedes, will you ride one day against Thebes? Your father's blood still hasn't been paid for."

"One day, but not yet. The battles are over but there's much to be done in Argos, and am I to see my home again only to leave it? If one day my grandfather should come back with his health restored, then the time would have come when I could lead men north to Thebes, and the sons of the other seven with me."

I reached the place where the two kings sat together in their diadems of gold and fine fringed tunics, and dropped on one knee before them. Diomedes bent forward to raise me to my feet, his face suddenly pitiful when he remembered my errand.

I put a long bundle wrapped in linen into his hands. The folds fell away and he held the lion dagger, tarnished from its week under the stones and wet flowers of Mycenae, but with the fighting men and running lions still clear and golden.

"So it was safe after all," said Leander, bending forward. "Diomedes, you never told me. I thought some Mycenean had it."

"Would I have let your gift fall into other hands?" asked Diomedes, smiling across at him. "Oh no, for the time being I am a king again and I must carry the king's sign with me always. Remember I haven't got a lion name like you."

He turned to the squire who was serving him. "Pour wine for Lord Hipponax."

163

"It used to be my duty to serve you," I said, as I sat down near the king's table.

"You have been more than a cupbearer in the history of Argos and Mycenae, Hipponax. Agamemnon won't forget that he might have died on the threshold of his father's hall if your shield hadn't been ready."

"Neither shall I," I said, looking at the bandaged arm where the long wound throbbed and itched. "Yet since the full moon I've fought four times in Argos and I think that's been the only moment when I did the right thing the first time."

The fire died low, and the maids cleared away the last of the banquet, while we sat, tired but contented, and talked a little of the last days. Then Leander limped up the stairway to the room where he had slept before and which seemed to belong to him now, and Diomedes' hand on my shoulder steered me out into the cool air of the great courtyard and up the steps to the south bastion.

A hush lay over Argos as the plain slept under the great stars, and Mecistheos greeted us quietly as he passed on his round of the guard. Diomedes rested his arms on the parapet.

"Now, for the first time, you are king of a country that's at peace," I said. "How does it feel?"

"I suppose you're right, I hadn't realized. So this is how it is to be a king! I'm glad I didn't know before or I shouldn't have had the courage to come to Argos."

"But it's what you wanted, what I trained you for?"

"Yes, Hipponax. The bird has flown from the nest and found out what wings are about! Still, if all the fighting hadn't come when it did I think I would have made a rather intolerable kinglet. I learned some things too fast, and some not fast enough."

"I couldn't help you, though I wanted to."

"Now, I suppose," he said, "that I shall rule here or in some other kingdom while my luck lasts."

"Not always in Argos?"

"No, Adrastus will come back, you know, and I shall be glad. Leander can rule alone, but learning to has changed him. I would be glad to serve a little longer under an older man before I live through anything like the last days again. Perhaps then I shall go out like my father and die in some strange land, but I shan't mind that as much as you would, because I should have had the same way of living and dying wherever I was."

"Diomedes, you know that if that day comes I won't be with you."

"Yes, I do know, but are you going to leave me now, Hipponax?"

"This morning I wasn't sure. Now I've seen my father. I must go to him, at least until he's more at peace about my brother's death."

"And then you can marry Chryseis!"

"I wouldn't have left you now for either of them, only you aren't a child any more; I think it might be better for you to have men around you who didn't know you when you were a small boy. And there's Leander." I remembered how I had seen the two young men together as I had come into the hall while Achates sang. I had known then that one part of my life was over and that I must lay it aside willingly lest I spoil the thing that I had made.

"Very well. In the morning you must make your plans. Dimini will be yours now, after your father, you know that, don't you? I shall never go back."

"Diomedes! Always we've only been stewards. The land was never ours."

"You heard the servants last night, 'Lord Hipponax'. A lord must hold land from his king, and in return he will owe certain duties, he and his children after him. Dark-haired sons, I should think, with eyes like Chryseis."

While I was still speechless, searching for words, he stood upright and yawned. "Let's go down, I could sleep for seven days. Oh Hipponax, look! Coming out of that trail of cloud; it's the night of the new moon."

HISTORICAL NOTE

It is natural to want to find out more about anything that we have found exciting, or that has interested us deeply. For many people the discovery of Greece and of the Greeks of the classical period has been this sort of experience, and they have wanted to know how it was that this people in their beautiful but difficult land came to create a way of life that can still influence us twenty-five centuries later. When we look beyond the Greece of Pericles and across the darkness and confusion of more than six hundred years we come to the Myceneans, whom we have named after their greatest citadel, Mycenae.

We cannot see them very clearly, and what we do know has come to us in two different ways. Firstly there are the legends and myths that were woven by Homer into his great poems, and used by most other Greek writers as the foundation of their work. Some scholars now believe that what were once thought to be no more than legends do in fact hold within them the names and some of the history of the kings and warriors who lived and fought between 1600 and 1200 B.C. and then disappeared from Greece as mysteriously as they came. In fact it was through the study of Homer that Schliemann the German archaeologist found the sites of both Mycenae of the High Kings, and Troy—the city across the Aegean sea that was sacked and burned by the most famous of those kings.

Schliemann and the others who followed him gave us the second window through which we can look into Mycenae when they uncovered the fallen walls and buried tombs with the gold and armour and wine cups of the Myceneans. These discoveries give us a very different picture of their way of life from Homer's. We learn from them that although the Myceneans did fight heroic battles and trade across the sea, their life at home was highly organized and their society more bound together by feudal responsibilities and duties than mediaeval England. Their kings, who not only ruled but also had some of the powers and responsibilities of priests, lived in great splendour, influenced in many ways, especially artistically, by the great Minoan civilization of Crete. They worshipped Gods who had not yet become those reverenced in the later temples of Delphi and Olympia. The most powerful were Potnia, mistress of animals and of all life, and particularly the goddess of women, and a warrior god who was known in his power over horses and bulls and the strong elements of life like earthquakes and storms at sea, and who later became Poseidon.

I have tried to look a few years back before the great campaign against Troy which was the climax of the Mycenean age, to imagine what might have happened before to some of the warriors who later fought there. At that time southern Greece was divided into at least four kingdoms of which the greatest was Mycenae, and the High King of Mycenae would have been the overlord of several little states—Argos, Tiryns, Corinth and others, each of which was no more than a few miles across. In Mycenae at this time the royal line of Atreus had been broken and I have imagined that something like this also happened at Argos. Adrastus, who had ruled there, seems from the legends to have been a man of strange moods and many adventures, and he was eventually succeeded not by a son but by the child of one of his daughters, Diomedes son of

Tydeos. Diomedes later became one of the most noble and courageous of the Greeks who fought before Troy, but you will not find Hipponax or Leander in the legends, or at least not under those names. When my story opens the siege of Troy is still ten years away and Diomedes of the loud war-cry is a boy of seventeen.

FAMILY TREE OF THE ROYAL HOUSE OF MYCENAE

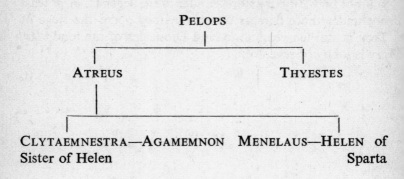

PELOPS

ATREUS   THYESTES

CLYTAEMNESTRA—AGAMEMNON   MENELAUS—HELEN of
Sister of Helen   Sparta

FAMILY TREE OF THE ROYAL HOUSE OF ARGOS

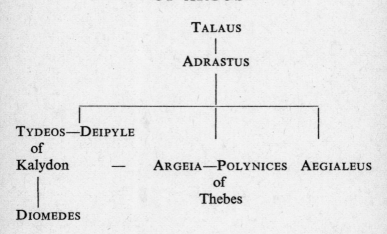

TALAUS

ADRASTUS

TYDEOS—DEIPYLE
of
Kalydon   —   ARGEIA—POLYNICES   AEGIALEUS
of
Thebes

DIOMEDES